Once Bitten, Twice Pie

Milly's Magical Midlife, Volume 3

Janet Butler Male

Published by Janet Male, 2021.

ONCE BITTEN, TWICE PIE

First edition. November 3, 2021.

Copyright © 2021 Janet Butler Male.

Written by Janet Butler Male.

Don't Wish for Murder

When I said I wanted more excitement, I didn't mean another murder. Or encounters with vampires. Or my dark secret biting me on the bum. As the saying goes, be careful what you wish for.

27th October 1987

In lovely Piddleton-on-Sea, Sussex, I was enjoying yet another day of leisure. Robbie, my new and gorgeous husband, was at his antique shop in nearby Brighton Lanes.

Apart from a brief maternity break when Kaye, my soon-to-be-married daughter, was born, I'd worked full time since I was sixteen. And in the last few months had solved two murders and rescued Kaye from an evil demon.

I know! Tell me about it.

From my comfy red sofa in the spacious, light-filled living room, I looked across the wide road at the pebble beach, the sea sparkling in October sunshine, and should have sighed with contentment. I'd recently sold my London flat for a fab price, given up my cafe, and it was bliss to have no money worries or responsibilities.

1

But instead of embracing leisure, I closed Sue Grafton's *C is for Corpse* and muttered, 'I could do with more excitement for real.'

What should I do that day? Perhaps nip into Brighton for a spot of shopping. No – I'd shopped till I dropped in the last few weeks and would soon need an entire room to store my clothes.

'Perhaps get a dog, take it for long walks,' I wondered out loud.

'Don't inflict a canine on me,' said Saphira, the beautiful 200-year-old talking cat, as she blinked her divine turquoise Oriental eyes. 'Pathetic to get a dog because you're bored. Besides, I can't abide their servility, stupid enough to run after sticks, balls and frisbees all day long. One of those silly drooling creatures will disturb my peace.'

'Don't be nasty, Saphira – dogs are cute.'

'Not as cute as me.'

'You're as cute as a she-devil.'

She cackled. 'I'm a bit prickly on the surface but have a heart of gold underneath.'

'Buried so deep it would take archaeologists to unearth it.'

Saphira had belonged to various witches and warlocks since she was born in Siam centuries earlier, only used her magic for good but enjoyed being catty. And her sarcasm, which she called *sarcatm*, was rubbing off on me.

I inherited her from my old boss and friend Prill, who I didn't know was a witch until she died, haunted me and asked me to find her murderer.

After masses of strange and unfortunate events, all now resolved, I'd recently married her son Robbie, and he didn't know of his mum's ghostly presence or magical history. Darling Prill still visited occasionally, popping up whenever and wherever.

The phone rang, and I crossed the deep-pile green carpet to the sideboard and picked up the receiver.

'Hi, Milly. It's me,' said a chirpy voice.

It was my friend and ex-business partner, Fawn. 'I thought you were in Thailand with Tarquin,' I said.

'I am – we're in Bangkok but fly back sometime this week.'

'That's rather vague.'

'Tell me about it – we were supposed to fly home yesterday, but Tarquin got his dates mixed up, and we're awaiting a cancellation.'

'With his money, you can hire a private jet or even buy one,' I quipped.

'I sometimes suspect Tarquin isn't as wealthy as he makes out. Anyway, are you enjoying your life of leisure?'

'It's great.'

'Liar. I can hear the boredom from here. Fancy starting a new business?'

'Still considering the costume jewellery idea.' I'd planned to open a costume jewellery shop in Brighton Lanes but kept putting it off. I told myself it was silly to sell fake jewels where many shop windows glittered with the real thing – both new and antique.

'But you're not keen?' Fawn said across the miles.

'Not really.'

'What are you doing this afternoon?'

'Nothing.'

'Good.'

'What's good about it?'

'You're free to check a cafe.'

'What cafe?'

'Listen up...'

Rich and Pour

As I put the phone down, I grinned stupidly.

'You resemble the Cheshire Cat,' said Saphira.

'Fawn has a great idea.'

'I heard the conversation – anything to stop you mooning around the house – a cat needs her privacy.'

Fawn's boyfriend owned many businesses in Brighton, including a department store and a few smaller concerns. One of the smaller concerns was Rich and Pour, a cafe on Union Street. Hamish, the current proprietor, was returning to Scotland, Tarquin had offered the cafe to Fawn and me at a low rent, and we had to decide fast.

As Fawn was away, return date unknown, the decision was mine.

'You have good intuition, Milly,' Fawn had said before she hung up, eager for a swim in the hotel pool. 'If the place feels good to you, phone me tomorrow as early as you like as we're about eight hours ahead here.'

'I'll call you either way, or you'll wonder.'

'Good. Yes, Tarquin, I'm coming. Go on ahead and order me a Mai Tai, and I'll shimmy into my swimsuit and be down in five. Don't forget to call me tomorrow, Milly.'

When I left for Brighton, Saphira was snoring gently on a sofa, curled up in a ball – unusual, as she usually slept splayed out, taking up as much space as possible.

I hadn't bothered with a car in London, but a week after moving to Piddleton-on-Sea, I treated myself to a new Jeep Wrangler. It took some getting used to, but I adored my soft-top funky yellow convertible, and as I drove along the seafront towards Brighton, the autumn wind in my hair, my heart lifted with delighted anticipation.

I'd thought that being married to a man who made my heart sing and having lots of free time would be heaven. But I missed a job to get up for in the mornings because leisure seemed less fun without the work contrast.

Turning off the seafront, I nosed the Jeep through narrow, busy streets into an underground car park near Brighton Lanes, which was an intriguing, quirky maze of twisting narrow alleyways, some of its buildings dating back to the 16th and 17th centuries. It was an 'Olde Worlde' film set and only a stone's throw from the beach.

After navigating the maze, I entered Rich and Pour on Union Street.

At first, it disappointed me as, despite its upmarket name, it was smaller and more downmarket than Scone but Not Forgotten – the London cafe Fawn and I briefly ran on King's Road, Chelsea. This place was more 'greasy spoon' than chic cafe. Gosh, how soon I'd become snobby after inheriting a London flat and a healthy back balance a few months earlier. Who did I think I was? Audrey Forbes Hamilton from *To the Manor Born*, perhaps. Or maybe Margot from *The Good Life*.

Get over yourself, Milly. I found a seat at a Formica-topped table in the cosy, smoke-filled cafe with a definite bohemian vibe and an eclectic mix of chatty, animated punters – all ages, all fashions. Billy Joel was belting out 'Uptown Girl' from four speakers set high on the terracotta walls.

On second thought, I loved the place.

There was no table service, so I popped my denim jacket over a chair back, approached the counter and studied the chalk-written menu on the rear wall. As I was about to order tea and a fruit scone, a waiter strode from the kitchen with a mountain of chips topped with melted cheese. It must have contained over a thousand calories. 'What's that dish, Rita?' I asked the woman behind the counter. I knew she was Rita because her name badge said so. *Miss Marple, eat your heart out.*

'It's our special – Cheesy Chip Mountain – fat and crispy French fries covered in strong melted cheddar cheese.'

I drooled. 'One of those and a mug of black tea, please.'

There goes the diet – again.

As a young teen, I stopped drinking tea with milk when Mum's mate served me a vomit-inducing beverage that was more milk than tea. Mum said I had to drink it, and I vowed never to risk it again.

Back at my table, I felt like a fat pig when a waiter served the young couple next to me with coffees and a tiny shortbread biscuit apiece.

I caught the woman's eye and said, 'You're sensible – I ordered the Cheesy Chip Mountain.'

She laughed. 'We're getting married soon, and my expensive dress is tight because of this place. The food is delicious.'

'My silly fiancée has no control and needs me to keep her in check,' said a pinch-faced man. 'We come in every morning and some afternoons, like today.'

'Do you have breakfast here?' I asked him.

'I don't allow breakfast.'

What a charmer. The pretty young woman reddened and shuffled in her seat. Almost lost for words, I regarded her and said, 'Do you work locally?'

'Yes. Simon has an estate agency, and I'm his secretary – Tuppence.'

'As in Agatha Christie's *Tommy and Tuppence*? I'm Milly, by the way.'

'Hello, Milly. Yes – Mum's always been a fan of the books. Have you seen the TV series, *Partners in Crime*?'

It was one of my favourites, and Francesca Annis, as Tuppence was gorgeous and wore the most divine hats and outfits. Tommy, played by James Warwick, wasn't half bad either. 'Yes, I love it,' I enthused.

Simon rolled his eyes. 'I have to see a man about a dog. See you in the office, Tuppence and don't waste time on silly female chitchat.'

Outrage erupted inside me, and I wanted to slap his smug face.

Tuppence fluttered her long eyelashes. 'Simon, I thought I'd food shop after this, then go straight home as I have that dinner party to prepare. Do you mind?'

He groaned. 'Can't get the staff.'

As he exited the cafe, my Cheesy Chip Mountain arrived.

'Can you help me out with these?' I asked Tuppence.

'I'd love to – don't tell Simon, or he'll kill me,'

'For eating a few chips?'

'For eating anything. When Simon had his tomato juice this morning, he allowed me a cup of coffee and said he doesn't want a fat wife.'

Allowed? 'There's nothing of you – you're a string bean.'

The blonde beauty clapped a hand to her full mouth. 'It was disloyal of me to diss Simon, but there's something about you that inspires confidences.'

The story of my life. My friend Prill, who was Robbie's mum – dead, a witch and a ghost, reckoned it was a superpower. 'When someone tells you something, nothing or nobody induces you to tell a living soul,' she'd said, or words to that effect.

Now I looked Tuppence directly in her large Disney-Princess blue eyes and said, 'Tell me whatever you want.'

I hadn't seen such beautiful eyes since … *don't go there, Milly* – I pushed the guilty memory away as usual.

After a moment's hesitation, Tuppence said, 'Simon says I've developed a tummy pouch, was skinnier when we got engaged, and I'm letting myself go.'

She popped a cheesy fat chip into her mouth, moaned with illicit culinary pleasure, then said, 'Simon has changed.'

'For the better?' I said, guessing the answer.

'Definitely for the worse. I want to escape him, but a powerful force won't let me.'

'What do you mean by worse? Is he violent?'

'No – just cold, controlling, calculating and money-mad. Before, Simon was only running the estate agency to appease his dad, but now seems obsessed.'

'Is his dad out of the picture?'

'Sort of – he retired to Phuket with his new Thai bride.'

'My friend, Fawn, is in Bangkok with her boyfriend.' I popped another succulent chip into my eager mouth.

'Tell her to keep him from the red-light area.'

I laughed.

'Don't laugh. Simon's parents were happy until they went to Phuket and his dad fell in love with a young woman who gave him a "healing massage". At first, he told his wife he wanted to rescue her, bring her to England, put her through university, but it was a ruse to keep her near. Within a year, he divorced his wife, signed over his business to Simon, lost twenty pounds, bought loads of designer swim and beachwear, then moved to Phuket where he runs a bar.'

Fascinated, I said, 'Is Simon's mum devastated?'

'No – euphoric. You must meet her – she's a hoot and rather cunning. She played the devastated wife card until a hefty divorce settlement was agreed. She also warned me against marrying Simon – or to at least wait a while as her son needs a battle-axe to control him, and I'm too sweet and compliant.'

I recalled my former lacklustre marriage, a symphony of over-politeness. But my ex was thriving with his new bossy and outspoken wife.

Remembering I was here to assess the cafe's potential, I said, 'What do you think about this place, Tuppence?'

'It's great – particularly in the mornings between eight and nine when everyone comes here before work. It's like a social club, and lots of business gets done amidst the gossip, frivolity and coffee cups. Although I hear the current proprietor is moving to Scotland with Rita, the love of his life, so I hope it doesn't become another antique shop or stuffy cafe.'

'Is there a stuffy cafe in Brighton Lanes?'

Tuppence groaned theatrically. 'Yes – Sweetie Pie, which has the cheer of a funeral parlour – the two cafes should swap names.'

'How do you mean?'

'*Sweetie Pie* sounds casual, approachable, *Rich and Pour* rather snobby, upmarket, but the former is full of joyless social climbers, and the atmosphere is frigid.'

I'd planned to keep it secret but said, 'My friend and I might run this place. We recently gave up a cafe on King's Road, Chelsea.'

Tuppence's mouth fell open. 'Not Scone but Not Forgotten?'

'The very one.'

'I've heard loads about it.'

'Good or bad?'

'Good, particularly the amazing shortbread – I heard it's magical.'

'Just a good recipe,' I lied. With the help of Saphira's magic, Fawn or I baked the shortbread with a drop of magical essence called Ojalis, which temporarily boosts mood and confidence.

I recalled Prill saying, 'The effect of Ojalis wears off but doesn't have the toxic effect of drugs and alcohol. Regular use trains the mind to be more optimistic, so eventually, it's unnecessary.'

Tuppence interrupted my reverie. 'So, will you buy Rich and Pour?'

'Probably just rent it. Anyway, I can't decide until I chat with Fawn.'

'Tarquin's new girlfriend?'

'Yes. How do you know?'

'Tarquin is Brighton royalty. He had a stable of admirers down here but dismissed them for Fawn. And there aren't many Fawns around.'

Gosh, I hadn't known about Tarquin's harem and doubted Fawn had either. But until recently, my friend hadn't been exactly faithful, so I would keep my mouth shut and not be a shot-dead messenger.

One gooey chip left on the plate, Tuppence and I eyed it. 'You have it,' I said.

'You have it,' parried Tuppence.

'No, you. I insist. My husband doesn't control my food intake.' The very idea – a husband who controlled my food intake would be dead or ex.

'Are you sure?' Tuppence licked her lips.

'Yes – go ahead.'

Practically drooling, she picked up the last fat chip and popped it in her mouth. 'Must go,' she said, mid-chew. 'I'm off to Marks and Spencer to buy dinner and must get home before Simon, so he doesn't see the boxes.'

This was insane. 'Simon doesn't know you buy ready-made food?'

'No – he thinks I'm a great cook. I dispose of the packaging and serve the food in Royal Crown Derby. Although funnily enough, he used to be a glutton, now just picks at his food. No wonder he's got skinny recently.'

Skinny? I don't think so.

Tuppence ferreted in her handbag, pulled out a photograph. 'I saw the look on your face. Check out this photo – Simon three months ago when he was slightly fatter but nicer.'

Slightly fatter? This Simon was at least three stones heavier than the Simon I'd seen earlier, and his cheekbones were lower, his hairline higher.

Odd.

As I mulled the difference, Tuppence popped the photo back in her bag and said, 'See you in the morning.'

'Did we make an appointment?' Gosh – I didn't mean to sound so formal.

'No – but pop here before 9 am, and your decision will be made.'

'What decision?'

'Whether to run this place.'

She sped away as I contemplated another Cheesy Chip Mountain.

No, Milly, just no. Besides, Robbie and I had plans for the local Indian restaurant, Currying Flavour, that evening, and I needed room for chicken tikka masala and its many delicious accompaniments.

Over a bottle of ice-cold Mateus Rose and ample amounts of curry and side dishes, I told Robbie about Rich and Pour.

Robbie had recently relocated his antique shop from Piddleton-on-Sea to Brighton Lanes. 'I usually go to Sweetie Pie for my morning coffee, but I'll join you tomorrow, Milly. Shall we drive into town together?'

About to say I'd take my Jeep, I considered my tight waistband and said, 'Yes, I'll come in with you, then walk home.'

He raised a doubtful brow. 'It's over five miles.'

'And I need the exercise.' I undid the top button of my jeans, which had been roomy a few weeks earlier. Perhaps I needed what Simon was on, but I hated the idea of going off my food. Although if I were genuinely disinterested in gluttony, maybe it wouldn't matter.

At school, I'd had a friend who was terrified of becoming a nun.

'Why would you do that? You only go to church because your mum makes you,' I said to the worried girl. 'What brought this on?'

'Mum's youngest cousin got the calling.'

'What calling?'

'God called her to become a nun.'

'Called her on the phone?' I joked.

'No, you dafty. Mum's cousin was watching *The Song of Bernadette* when she heard God's voice.'

'What did He say?'

'Hilda, devote your life to the church and become a nun.'

'Did she?'

'Yes. What if that happens to me?'

'It won't.'

'Are you sure? I'd look awful in a habit.'

'Positive – I swear on my budgie's life you'll never be a nun.'

Perhaps I took Joey's name in vain as he fell off his perch three weeks later, but my friend never became a nun. Last I checked, she had three children and worked in Woollies.

What got me on that train of silly thought? Oh, Robbie's concern that I might go off my food – fat chance – more chance of me going up a dress size or three.

'You're miles away.' Robbie took my hand across the table.

'Thinking of becoming a nun.'

'Don't you dare – I doubt convents have conjugal rights visits.'

'Is that all you care about?'

'Hardly. You also make a fine apple pie.'

I laughed. 'Talking about puddings, have we room for mango kulfi?'

'Always.'

The Bully

28th October 1987

The following day, we drove to Brighton in Robbie's white convertible Aston Martin. After he stowed his pride and joy in a safe corner of the underground car park, we strolled hand-in-hand to Rich and Pour. When we entered the riotous, convivial atmosphere, we were lucky to get a free table.

As we flopped onto red vinyl chairs, I noticed we were next to Tuppence and Simon.

'Hello again,' said Tuppence in a strained tone before looking bleakly at a half-eaten slice of dry toast.

Was that a bruise on her neck? No, perhaps a love bite and Simon was more passionate than he looked.

I fancied a sausage and fried egg sandwich with lashings of brown sauce along with a mug of tea but felt bad ordering such deliciousness in front of Tuppence.

'Come on, Tuppence, you've had enough food, and it's greedy to eat until lunchtime. Grab your coat and my takeaway coffee, and let's go.'

'Can I have a takeaway coffee, Simon?' she said.

Fancy having to ask.

'No – because you won't drink it black and don't need the milk calories.'

Simon said no.

As Robbie and I exchanged outraged glances, poor Tuppence muttered a hasty farewell and scurried after Simon.

'What a bully,' said Robbie. 'Is it table service?'

'No – order at the counter – we're not at the Ritz.'

'Perhaps not – but there's loads of wealth in this place.' He nodded towards tables laden with jewellery, wads of cash, and small antiques.

A small pixie-like man with a wide grin sat at the vacated table and said, 'Us dealers do loads of business here. I'm Terry of Terry's Treasures.'

'Robbie of Retro Relics and this is Milly, my wife,' said Robbie. 'I recently relocated from Piddleton-on-Sea.'

'Where business was probably piddling – you're in the right place now – we scratch each other's backs here, and it boosts business. Take yesterday at Bermondsey market – I spotted a diamond engagement ring at a diamond price. Now, my shop doesn't sell jewellery, so I'll sell it to Derek.'

He pointed at a slim, elegant man deep in conversation with a pretty red-headed woman. 'I'll turn an immediate profit, and he'll turn a profit when he sells it at retail to some besotted couple, and he'll then give me a percentage of the profits.'

'Couldn't you sell it to a besotted couple, cut out the middleman?' I said, confused.

'Not for the same money as his shop is highfalutin, all glittery rings, bracelets and stuff. My place isn't posh enough.'

I was getting it. 'Will Derek do the same for you?'

'Of course, he found a Victorian vase at an estate sale last week, sold it to me, then I flogged it to some old dame dripping in dosh and gave Derek a percentage.'

To Robbie, he said, 'My mate wanted to rent your new shop, but you pipped him to the post. If you move out, he'll give you a back-hander.'

Robbie's tummy rumbled loudly, and Terry said, 'Mine's about to follow. Give us your orders, and I'll nip to the counter.'

'I'll go,' I said.

'No – I insist.'

Over delicious sausage and fried egg sandwiches dripping with butter and brown sauce, Terry told us about local life and business. It sounded like a fairytale. 'Are all the local business people good to deal with and honest?' I asked.

'In the main, darling, as in such a tight-knit community, you'd be outed in a flash and ostracised.' Then he looked at Robbie and said, 'What do you specialise in?'

'This and that.'

'Best to specialise, mate. Anything you find on your travels that doesn't fit your MO, you can flog in one of the Brighton Lanes shops. Just ask me, and I'll point you in the right direction.'

'What do the other dealers specialise in?' I said.

Terry rubbed his chin. 'Silver; clocks and watches; lamps and chandeliers; gold and silver jewellery; silver jewellery only; gold jewellery only. Two shops are vintage – one sells pre-1950s clothes and accessories, the other old newspapers, books and magazines.'

A dark cloud passed over Terry's cheeky face. 'Then there's the shop we all avoid.'

The ominous tone made my tummy churn. 'Which is?'

He reddened, cleared his throat. 'It sounds daft, but we're all wary of a shop called Transylvanian Trinkets. The same person who has Books and Bites in Piddleton-on-Sea is the proprietor.'

I'd passed Books and Bites the previous day, although some dark, invisible force-field stopped me going in. It was on the premises which had been Robbie's Retro Relics. Someone had offered Robbie a reasonable price for it recently, and he accepted. But when he told me, my blood froze, especially when he confirmed the purchaser had a defined Eastern European appearance with honed features, high cheekbones, dark hair and a widow's peak.

When Prill first met Saphira in 1976, she (the cat) was trapped in a shop the previous owner (a vampire) had planned to call Books and Bites, and his intentions were evil.

Saphira put many obstacles in the vampire's way, and he disappeared, and the premises became Prill's final earthly business – Baking and Entering. Then Robbie turned it into Retro Relics, and it was now Books and Bites – full circle.

'Who runs Books and Bites?' Robbie said.

'Tallon's nephew,' replied Terry.

I gulped. 'So Tallon is the vampire, I mean, man, who purchased the Piddleton-on-Sea premises?'

Terry frowned. 'Did you say vampire?'

'No – empire.' Gosh, the lies rolled off my tongue. 'What's Tallon's nephew called?' I said to divert attention.

'William. Oh, look – he's here.'

A tall, skinny man, average looking, wearing pale foundation and black eyeliner, minced through the door – Marilyn Monroe's wiggly walk was manly in comparison. Frightened-rabbit eyes belied his air of bravado.

'Watcha, William,' shouted Terry. 'Order a coffee and join us.'

'Don't mind if I do,' said William in a high-pitched voice, redolent of John Inman from *Are You Being Served?*

William wiggled to the counter, placed his order, wiggled towards us as if on a fashion-show catwalk, lowered himself onto the chair opposite Terry and crossed his long legs as I got a strong whiff of Giorgio Beverly Hills.

'Did you get that first edition of *Gone with the Wind* for Audrey?' Terry said.

'Right here.' William handed over a Harrods bag. 'I tucked the invoice into the book.' Then he grinned, and my tummy clenched as I spied a small pair of fangs, or at least sharp eye teeth.

As Rita delivered William's tomato juice, she knocked over Terry's half-full glass of orange juice, and it smashed.

'Oh, I'm so sorry,' she said. 'I'll grab a cloth and a mini dustpan and brush.'

William pulled a large red handkerchief from a pocket of his tight black leather jacket and picked up the broken glass as a sharp shard pierced his skin and caused his finger to bleed, and he squealed, 'Oh, no. I can't stand the sight of blood – oh, the room is spinning.'

Then he slid from his chair and onto the red linoleum floor with a crash as everyone gasped.

William couldn't be a vampire if he fainted at the sight of blood.

Could he?

Could It Be Murder?

By presumably sheer coincidence, Tallon was passing as William fainted. I knew it was him because Robbie hissed in my ear, 'That's the man who bought the Piddleton-on-Sea premises.'

Spotting William in a heap on the floor, Tallon strode in, creating a chilly atmosphere of menace, scooped his nephew up and carried him from the cafe as if rescuing a damsel in distress. In what he obviously thought was a whisper, he said, 'How dare you embarrass me, Villiam – I von't stand for it – I bet you fainted at the sight of blood again.'

'You didn't say Tallon's rather handsome,' I whispered to Robbie.

Rather handsome? Ha! Try Drop-dead gorgeous. He had an elegant long-limbed figure, and his face was fine-boned with an aquiline nose, high cheekbones you could sharpen knives on, and a firm manly jaw with a hint of stubble. And the eyes – piercing green come-to-bed vibrant peepers. And he'd smelt of cedarwood and sex.

Dangerous – and I realised how easy it was to succumb to a vampire's dark charms. Then I imagined lying undead in a coffin and shook myself to sense. What was I thinking? Gorgeous Robbie was the love of my life.

I'd almost lowered my collar and rushed after Tallon, neck bared, right there in Brighton Lanes. 'Take me now, Tallon.'

Of course, I didn't share my fantasy with Robbie, who said, 'Must go. See you later, darling.'

He gently kissed my mouth and made a swift exit.

Moments later, Tuppence ran into the cafe wild-eyed and hissed at me, 'Come quick, Milly – Simon is dead.'

Oh no, not again. Earlier that year, someone rushed into Scone but Not Forgotten and asked me to come quickly as her husband had just died.

Why me again?

Last time, the victim's wife hadn't even called the police.

'What happened?' I said as we sped from the cafe.

'I'll tell you when we get there – hurry.'

'Did you call a doctor?'

No answer.

'Have you called the police?' I said as we dashed towards Meeting House Lane.

'Not yet,' she shouted over her shoulder. 'I panicked and thought you'd help.'

Despite the old building, Simon's office, above a sandwich shop, was a streamlined shiny affair full of Conran furniture and expensive Andy Warhol prints – or were they the real thing?

Behind the glass-topped desk, Simon lay open-eyed and dead beneath a silver-framed print (or original painting) of Debbie Harry.

'What happened?' I asked the terrified Tuppence.

'He had a sort of fit, clutched his heart, then fell. His breathing was ragged – then he foamed at the mouth and died.'

'What were his final words?'

'Final word – AAAAAAAAAARRRRRRRRRRGH!'

'I don't see any foam.'

'I wiped it away with a tissue.'

'Where's the tissue?'

'In the bin.' Tuppence pointed towards a chrome waste paper bin, then crumpled onto a blue suede sofa, saying, 'He said I'd be the death of him – maybe it was my fault.'

As Tuppence was a useless crying mush, I picked up the phone and dialled 999.

'Fire, police or ambulance?' said an efficient female voice.

I explained the situation, and she said the police would be along soon.

I've watched too many detective shows and read too many mysteries and expected one handsome detective with a plain sidekick or vice versa. And, shame on me, I expected two men.

But two women arrived – one chic, coiffed, fiftyish and fragrant with Chanel No. 5, the other a scruffy young woman with messy ginger hair, freckles and a baggy creased suit, emanating Eau de Damp Clothes.

The older woman held out an elegant hand that boasted perfectly manicured shell-pink nails. 'I'm Detective Inspector Joan Forbes, and this is my assistant, Detective Sergeant Nelly Slocombe. Call us DI Forbes and DS Slocombe if you would be so kind. Now, where is the body?'

Some detective, but perhaps she was just being polite. I motioned behind the desk.

'What happened?' said DI Forbes.

'He had a fit then dropped dead,' I said.

'Are you his girlfriend?'

'Just a friend, but his fiancée is too upset to speak.'

DI Forbes did a few rudimentary checks of Simon's body. 'Looks like death by natural causes, but the doctor, on his way, will confirm.'

As Tuppence was a snivelling mess on the sofa, I said, 'Should I stay?'

DI Forbes regarded me with cold but beautiful grey eyes. 'Did you witness the event?'

Due to Tuppence's imploring glance, I hesitated. 'Er, not exactly. I was in Rich and Pour, and Tuppence ran to get me, said Simon was dead, and we sped here, called 999, and you were here within minutes.'

As DI Forbes picked up a takeaway cup, I thought she was about to sniff the contents, but she put it to her lips.

Yuck. Who picks up someone's discarded coffee and drinks it?

As my tummy heaved at the thought, Tuppence shouted, 'Stop – don't drink that.'

DI Forbes' eyes widened, but she returned the cup to the glass-topped chrome desk and said, 'Why shouldn't I drink my coffee?'

DS Slocombe cleared her throat. 'Erm, that's not your coffee, ma-am. I put yours on the side table.'

'You've rather landed yourself in it, young lady.' DI Forbes glared at Tuppence. 'Why didn't you want me to drink that coffee?'

Tuppence stuttered, 'Erm, Simon likes, I mean liked, his coffee very strong.'

'A likely tale. Tell me the entire story, young lady.'

'Shall I stay?' I said, knowing the answer.

DI Forbes shook her perfectly coiffed head dismissively. 'Absolutely not – write your name, address and telephone number in this notebook, then please leave. I have no wish for amateur Miss Marples, young, old, middle-aged or otherwise.'

That was me told, so I reluctantly left as I heard the scruffy one say to Tuppence, 'Can I get you a cup of tea and a biscuit, love?'

Vampires and Suchlike

Not ready to return home, I dashed to Robbie's shop, where he sat behind his mahogany desk with a face as long as a horse's.

'Simon's dead,' I said, but Robbie didn't answer, obviously wrapped in thought.

'Simon's dead,' I repeated.

'Did Tuppence kill him?'

'Why would you say that?'

'The poor mite seemed terrified of him. What happened?'

I told him, but he still seemed miles away.

'What's the matter?' I said.

'I'm not up for it.'

'Up for what?'

'Brighton Lanes. I wished I'd kept the shop in Piddleton-on-Sea.'

I sat in a gilt chair opposite his leather-topped desk and took his hand. 'But why?'

'It's so specialised here in Brighton Lanes, and I don't have adequate antique knowledge. My former shops were more bric-à-brac, and I blagged my way around but won't get away with that here.'

'Do something less specialised,' I suggested.

'Like what?'

'You said you liked my idea of retro costume jewellery, and it's all the rage since the Duchess of Windsor's jewellery sale in Geneva. Is that what you secretly want to do?'

Gosh – I hope not as it's not very manly.

'No.'

Phew. 'What do you rather do?'

'Deal in classic cars.'

That's more like it.

'Are you sure?'

If he keeps chopping and changing, he'll get dizzy.

A big grin creased his face. 'Definitely, and you won't believe how much Terry offered me for the Aston Martin. I've made thousands in a few months – I told you it was a fantastic investment.'

When he named the sum, I almost followed William in a dead faint.

'That's not all,' Robbie added. 'Terry's mate offered me a few grand to move out of these premises by the end of the week, and Terry has already bought my stock. So, it's Robbie's Classics, here I come.'

'Where will you run the business from?'

'Home.'

That clinched it – I needed a job. Husbands are great, but not under your feet all day.

But his enthusiasm was infectious, and I was happy for him but anxious about Tuppence.

After the long walk home to clear my head, I was glad to fall onto a sofa beside Saphira.

'Don't get too comfy,' she said, 'The phone will ring in a moment, says my extra-sensory...'

'Yes, Saphira – your extra-sensory cat perception – no need to finish the sentence.'

'But you just did.'

'Did what?'

'Finished the sentence. Why is it okay for you to discuss my extra-sensory cat perception and not me?'

'I give up,' I said as the phone rang, and Saphira gave an I-told-you-so grin.

'So, what do you think?' Fawn breathed down the crackly line.

'About what?' I said, playing for time.

'Shall we take over Rich and Pour?'

I wasn't sure – half of me wanted a quieter life, and the other half was charmed and seduced by the cafe's crazy busy vibe.

'Decide soon as the other interested party is pressuring Tarquin like crazy.'

'Dangling expensive carrots before him?' I said.

'Probably yes. Shall we grab the chance, Milly?'

Undecided, I took advantage of Saphira's extra-sensory cat perception. Covering the mouthpiece, I looked into her beautiful eyes and said, 'Should Fawn and I take over Rich and Pour?'

Saphira gazed back. 'The sparkle in your eyes says yes, so there's your answer.'

Despite Saphira's assurance, I didn't want the decision to rest solely on my shoulders, so I said, 'Before I answer, Fawn, what's your vibe as your intuition is better than mine.'

Prill had said we both had superb intuition, but Fawn had a side of psychic.

'My brilliant intuition says yes,' she said.

'Then my answer is yes.'

Fawn whooped.

When I replaced the receiver, I said to Saphira, 'I agreed to the cafe. Have I done the right thing?'

'You tell me.'

'You said to say yes.'

'If I told you to stick your hand in the fire, would you?' Saphira retorted.

'Ha! That's what the teachers in infant school said.'

'Quite – stop behaving like an infant.'

'Have I done the right thing?' I repeated.

'What do you think?'

'I'm not sure.'

'Imagine how you'd feel if you turned down Rich and Pour and someone else nabbed it.'

I buried my head in my hands, thought hard and imagined the scenario.

'Well?' said Saphira as I looked up again. 'What's the verdict?'

'I'd regret it.'

'Good. And my tummy will regret it if you don't fetch my smoked salmon and prawns – with a squeeze of lemon and served on my favourite plate.'

'Yes, your majesty, coming up. Would you like champagne with it?'

Saphira waved a dismissive paw. 'Pah – I only drink alcohol at weddings. I'll have a small bowl of Evian water alongside.'

I carefully prepared Saphira's little feast in the kitchen and placed a sprig of catnip on the plate. Then I took it to her mini-Chippendale table and chair and popped a Bach CD into the stereo.

As the soothing tones permeated the room, she said, 'Not Bach today – Mozart.'

I did as bid, then said, 'Enjoy your snack, Saphira – I'm off upstairs for a nap.'

She licked her lips. 'Then we'll discuss murder, vampires and suchlike. What time is Robbie home?'

'I'm not sure, but he said he might go out with Terry, his new best mate, tonight.'

'Make sure he does. It's tedious that he thinks I'm a normal cat – look at me – such superior gorgeousness isn't normal.'

'Your modesty humbles me, Saphira.'

'What do I have to be modest about? Now, go away; my smoked salmon is getting warm.'

With an amused grin, I left her to it, went upstairs, threw off my clothes, popped on a dressing gown, flopped onto the bed and wondered about poor Tuppence. Could she have murdered Simon?

I doubted it but realised I didn't have her phone number or address, and if I phoned the police station, it might seem suspicious. 'Er, hello, I phoned emergency services about a dead body earlier. Do you know where Tuppence is?'

That could land me in a mess I didn't want – yet again.

Without boring you with too much backstory, since I got divorced earlier that year, I'd solved two murders and travelled back in time to the Regency period to solve the second.

Enough was enough, and I had no wish to be embroiled again, so why did intuition say I would be?

I heard the front door slam, and Robbie's footsteps padded up the stairs.

'Hello, darling,' he said. 'Have you heard more about Tuppence? I'm sorry I was distracted earlier – it was probably the shock

– you don't expect to see someone hail and hearty one minute, then dead the next.'

'I know – it's awful.'

'By the way, you spoil that cat – she's at her mini mock-Chippendale dining suite.

Little did Robbie know it wasn't faux Chippendale but the real thing. So perhaps it was fortuitous for him to switch from antiques to classic cars.

'Are you out with Terry tonight?' I said.

'Do you mind? He wants to discuss my Aston Martin before he gives me a cheque. And he reckons he can connect me with loads of people who want cars but have no time to search.'

'Fine – as long as we have a lovely romantic dinner later this week.'

I was careful not to sound like I wanted to push him out, but I was desperate to talk to Saphira.

'What shall I wear?' he said.

I raised one eyebrow, a trick he'd taught me. 'Do you fancy Terry?'

'Don't be daft.'

It often surprised me how unconfident Robbie could be, despite his parents being the confident Prill and Bill.

Not only was Robbie's mum a ghost witch, but his dad was also a ghost warlock; Robbie had no clue, and it was tricky to keep schtum.

I could tell he was genuinely concerned about what to wear, so I said, 'Your black Levi 501s with your lightweight blue cashmere sweater and the black blazer.'

'Thanks, darling.' He kissed my cheek and said, 'Mind if I have the first shower?'

'Go ahead, as long as I can watch. I'm having a night in with a video.'

'Which one?'

'No idea – if there's nothing suitable in the cupboard, I'll stroll to the local Blockbuster and choose. I quite fancy *Withnail and I* or *Ruthless People*.'

'My vote is *Aristocats*,' whispered Saphira, unheard by Robbie.

When he was ready and fragranced with the divine Sultry Sandalwood, I wanted to rip his clothes off but restrained myself. 'Have a good time, Robbie darling, but resist the raw onions or sex is off the table.'

'I'd rather have it on the table.'

'Naughty boy – you know what I mean.'

'Yes – and I'll resist the raw onions. See you later.'

'Are you off now?'

'Yes, we're meeting in the Grand for a bottle of champers first. I'll leave the car at Terry's, grab a cab home.'

'Have a great time.'

As he dashed around getting ready, I contemplated how different life was since my divorce. Steve and I had rarely gone anywhere separately, and it was stifling.

After the Aston Martin's melodious V8 engine burbled away, I had a quick shower, pulled on my favourite blue cotton pyjamas and my old candlewick dressing gown and went downstairs to join Saphira, now on a plush gold pillow atop a sofa.

'Did you enjoy your nap?' she said.

Gosh – something was in the air – Saphira being nice. 'Did you enjoy your smoked salmon?'

'Always. What will you eat?'

'Cheddar cheese and cream crackers with dollops of Branston pickle.'

I enjoyed being home alone occasionally, so I didn't have to eat a full dinner. It was good for my psyche and my waistline.

'You seem calm,' said Saphira.

'About what?'

She blinked her mesmerising eyes. 'Well, a murder for one.'

Half Bitten

'What murder?' I said.

'Simon's,' replied Saphira.

'We don't know he was murdered.'

'Yes, we do – you can sense it, and so can I.'

Unfortunately, she was right – and I *was* strangely calm. During the first murder investigation, I was constantly restless, the second less so, and perhaps I'd become blasé, but maybe it would be different if I were the suspect. That must be awful. And during the last murder investigation, the life of my beloved daughter Kaye was under threat from an evil demon, which gave me a turbo-charged impetus to solve the case.

Compared to that, nothing could be so awful.

Then I remembered the vampires, and my heart skipped a beat. Could they be involved?

'You just thought of vampires,' said Saphira.

'How do you know?'

'You're as pale as Dracula.'

'Why do we need a conversation?' I said. 'I'll just sit here while you read my mind.'

'That would be boring.'

'Yes, it would.'

Saphira flicked her tail. 'Shall we discuss matters, make a plan?'

'Yes – where shall we begin?'

'By calling Prill.'

'I thought she was off-limits for a while.' I'd had strict instructions only to summon her in an emergency.'

Saphira smirked. 'If this isn't an emergency, I don't know what is.'

'Simon's probable murder, you mean?'

'Yes, and the fact we have a huge vampire problem which your new cafe might help solve, that's why I encouraged you to go ahead.'

'How could my cafe help?'

'Vampires are taking over Brighton, and their dark force can make people negative and vindictive. You know that bonhomie and mutual back-scratching Terry discussed earlier?'

'How do you know what he said?'

'You told me.'

'Oh, I remember now, Saphira.' I wasn't sure I did, but whatever.

'That'll go if we don't act fast. Vampires don't just suck blood; they suck positive energy from people. When you run the cafe, and everyone has magic shortbread with their teas and coffees, it will help elevate positivity, offset the negative vampire energy.'

'I see your point.'

'Call Prill now,' urged Saphira.

'How?'

'The same spell as last time.'

Ah yes, the one I was only to use in an emergency.

My calm demeanour disappeared, and my heart drummed in my ears. If Prill was willing to be dragged from a long romantic sojourn with Bill, this must be serious, and Saphira knew more than she was admitting to.

As usual.

Nervously I said the magic words, 'Prithee Prill, come to me,' and she appeared in a fragrant cloud of jasmine, gorgeous as ever in a red Jaeger trouser suit and silk leopard-print blouse with a pussy-cat bow.

'I hope this is important,' she said. 'Bill and I were in Sorrento eating delicious porcini risotto.'

Sometimes life (and death) isn't fair. Although Prill was dead, a witch and a ghost, she and her equally dead husband had a special spell that enabled them to eat and drink like humans for a few days each month.

I knew we should discuss important stuff but couldn't resist saying, 'What did you have for starters?'

'Baked figs with blue cheese – heaven.'

'And what did you plan for pudding?'

'Tiramisu.'

Dreaming of food, I told Prill about Tuppence and Simon. What was wrong with me? 'Why is food foremost in my mind when mayhem and murder are in the air?' I muttered.

'Avoidance tactic,' said Saphira. 'Some divert themselves with food when deep problems are afoot; others avoid it. Also, you're imagining a four-cheese pizza followed by a big bowl of chocolate ice cream.'

I was. 'Since when could you read my mind?'

'It's intermittent and more apparent near full-moon nights.'

Prill tutted. 'Milly, if you're unaccustomed to Saphira's powers by now, I'm disappointed.'

Gosh, Prill seemed miffed we'd dragged her away from Bill and their delicious dinner- she rarely sounded snooty and annoyed. But perhaps I was selfish, and she had problems. 'Are you okay, Prill? You don't seem yourself.'

'I'm sorry, Milly. Bill and I were having a little tiff. He wants us to leave this realm forever, and I want to nip in and out – see Robbie – and you, of course.'

'What about me?' said Saphira.

'Don't be silly – you can travel to any realm you want whenever you want.'

Wow – I didn't know that. Perhaps Saphira had a smidgeon of modesty after all.

Swallowing a lump in my throat, I said, 'Where would you go if you left us, Prill?'

'Nirvania – heaven for dead witches and warlocks who've accomplished a certain amount of good deeds.'

Saphira tensed then tucked in her tail. 'This is no time for silly chatter – we have problems. Milly, tell Prill about Simon's possible murder.'

I did.

'Whether a natural or suspicious death, sounds like he deserved it, as I despise bullies,' said Prill after I finished my spiel.

Out of character, Saphira said, 'Everyone is innocent until proven guilty. I feel vampires or other dark forces caused Simon's change of character and caused his death.'

'How do you know he changed character?' I said.

Saphira rolled her eyes. 'You told me.'

'Did I?' I honestly couldn't remember.

Everything seemed out of sync. Prill was never snappy; Saphira was usually judgmental. What was going on? Something was in the air, and it wasn't good – I sensed menace.

'Vampires are taking over Brighton, and we must stop them because last time Tallon was so powerful, he drained my powers,' said Saphira.

Prill clutched her slender throat. 'He's definitely the same vampire you thwarted last time, Saphira darling?'

'Yes – it was the first time I'd felt vulnerable in over a hundred years.'

I felt vulnerable at least once a day, but I wasn't a 200-year-old talking cat, nor did I want to be. Then again, Saphira had a rather good life.

'Is Tallon the worst of the lot, Saphira?' I said.

'Yes, and probably the ringleader.'

The ringleader? That sounded bad. 'How many are there?'

Saphira counted on her claws. 'Well, there's Tallon, his nephew, and I suspect Simon was a vampire before his demise.'

'I thought they needed stakes through their hearts to die.'

Prill interjected. 'That's only for long-established vampires, and, besides, there are other ways to slay them. Fresh vampires or half vampires can die of natural or nasty causes.'

'What's a half-vampire?' I said.

'One who was bitten with one fang, or both fangs only grazed the skin's surface.'

'What about a fresh half-bitten vampire?' I said – half because I was interested, half to be cheekily difficult.

Prill tutted. 'You did maths at school – work it out.'

'Ah, so a half-bitten fresh vampire is a quarter-vampire.'

'Give that woman a gold star,' said Prill.

But I didn't understand how a vampire could bite with only one fang, and Saphira reread my mind. 'Tallon's left fang developed an abscess, and he needed a root canal and a crown, but fortunately for his victims, the replaced fang doesn't extend when he's in full vampire mode, so his bite is only half effective.'

'Surely he didn't go to a regular dentist?'

'No – a vampire dentist,' said Saphira.

'Do you mean a dentist who is a vampire or a dentist who treats vampires?'

'Both.'

'Where does he or she practice?'

'Transylvania.'

How did Saphira know all this, and why had she kept it quiet? So I asked her the same.

Books and Bites

'Well, it's like this,' Saphira began. 'In the 1970s, I was unfortunate enough to fall into Tallon's clutches. He was so charming that he even fooled clever me. I stupidly believed his fangs were pointed eye teeth, and he was a good warlock. For two years, we toured the world, stayed in the best hotels – I was his beloved familiar. A terrible toothache in a fang sent him screaming to Transylvania and the dentist. That's when I realised he was a vampire, not a warlock.'

'Did you accompany him, Saphira?'

She flattened her ears against her head and bared her teeth. 'Yes – that's when I became his virtual prisoner. When we returned to England, he told me of his evil plan – from small and discreet premises in Piddleton-on-Sea, he would open a cafe-cum-bookshop called Books and Bites. It would be an innocent-looking front for a hostile takeover bid. He wanted vampires first to rule Brighton, then Sussex, then Britain, then Europe, then the entire world.'

'But you had a counter-attack plan?'

'Yes – in Transylvania, I snuck into the castle library and, with the help of a vengeful witch servant, found an ancient book which told me how to thwart Tallon's powers. I bided my time until we were back in Piddleton-on-Sea, unleashed the magic, but the spell was so powerful I temporarily lost my energy and became nearly a normal cat, albeit spectacularly beautiful – but, oh, the shame.'

Prill stroked Saphira's back lovingly. 'At great risk to herself, this darling cat finally scuppered Tallon's powers, leaving her weak and near death. After Tallon fled, I found her in the Piddleton-on-Sea premises.'

'Then you bought it and turned it into Baking and Entering, Prill?' I confirmed.

'Yes. That's it.'

'So why is Tallon back, and aren't you worried he'll want revenge, Saphira?' I said.

'He probably has no idea I am still alive and that I incanted the spell to thwart his powers.'

Confused, I rubbed my forehead. 'Why would Tallon return to Sussex? Why start again where he failed before?'

'Ego,' said Saphira. 'Vampires can't bear to fail.'

Neither can many humans and a certain cat.

Prill clapped her hands noiselessly. 'Let's not dwell on the past, but forge ahead with the current problems. Milly, would you summarise what you know before you investigate, although Saphira and I will help magically in the background.'

I shouldn't be churlish, but why me again? Why was this my responsibility? I tried to stay calm, but anger surged through my veins. 'I don't want to be involved – not with vampires – not with solving Simon's murder. Why me?'

With a kind smile, Prill said, 'Milly, you are the most open-minded human

I know. As a ghost, I can only do so much, and as a cat, Saphira can't make enquiries and do detective work, but when Fawn returns, she'll help you.'

'Suppose so,' I mumbled.

I guessed Saphira and Prill could do more than they admitted – however, I wasn't starting an argument I would probably lose.

Prill tutted. 'Why the reluctance, Milly?'

Where to start? 'Last time was easier – if I didn't solve the murder, a demon would have caused my daughter's demise. The need to save Kaye gave me incredible energy and staunched my fear.'

Prill fiddled with her pearls. 'If you don't stop these dangerous vampires in their tracks, good people, your daughter included, will have unhappy futures, ruled by evil entities. Let's catch this problem before it escalates horrifically. The first step is to save Tuppence. Please fetch the crystal ball to see what her future will be if we don't intervene.'

I sighed. 'Where is the crystal ball this time?'

'The usual place – the middle shelf in your wardrobe.'

'Last time, it was in my London wardrobe, and I didn't see the crystal ball when I packed my belongings.'

Prill grinned. 'It's like a homing pigeon.'

I rescued the crystal ball from a shelf in my Piddleton-on-Sea wardrobe – wrapped in a purple silk cover. It was an extra-special magical sphere that could see the past and future, but it only showed scenarios relevant to current problems. Downstairs, I placed it on the coffee table, and Prill looked into its depths as I sat with Saphira on my lap.

As Prill gazed, she emitted an awful groan. 'We must act fast on Tuppence's behalf.'

'Why?' I said.

Prill gave me a piercing glance. 'Is there something you haven't told me, Milly?'

As my tummy quivered, I lifted my chin defiantly – had Prill uncovered my terrible secret? 'How do you mean?'

Prill bit her lip, hesitated, then said, 'As you know, the magic globe shows the past if events are relevant. Normally I'd employ tact about delicate matters, but as time is of the essence, I'll be direct.'

I clutched at my pyjama top as Saphira said, 'I'm a cat on a hot tin roof here – spill, Prill.'

Time raced backwards, and my heart thumped loudly in my ears as Prill said, 'Why didn't you say you gave your baby up for adoption, Milly? You know I'd have understood. But you told me it died.'

Buried Secrets

In the spring of 1964, I was working for Prill.

From my first day in Togs boutique in Liverpool the previous year, she was my fairy godmother. I was only sixteen, but she treated me with respect, even took me on a London buying trip where we stayed in the Dorchester hotel. She promised to take me to France and Italy. 'Boulogne is wonderful for cheap and fabulous clothes, darling. And Paris is divine. We'll stay in the George Cinq.'

Prill also adored my boyfriend Mike, and she sometimes wined and dined us in Liverpool's top restaurants when Bill, her husband, was away. Mike believed me capable of anything, as did Prill. They were heady and happy days.

Mike and I often discussed 'going abroad' – a big thing at the time. We spent hours in coffee bars discussing imaginary trips.

One day, in the Kardomah cafe on Bold Street, he slapped me in the face – not literally – when he said, 'I'm off to Valencia with my mates next week.'

Upset and lost for words, I looked down at my black and white mini skirt as he took my hand and said, 'Are you alright, Milly?'

A fat tear plopped onto the harlequin print, and I was too choked to speak.

After a while, I managed a shaky, 'But our plans...'

'It's too good an opportunity to miss, Milly. John's dad has a Spanish apartment, and I only need airfare and spending money.'

As blood thumped in my ears, I saw red, rose from the table and dashed from the cafe in floods of tears, unpursued by Mike.

To Prill's despair, I moped around in Togs until she said, 'What on earth is the matter, Milly?'

When I told her, she frowned. 'But Mike's only eighteen – give the lad some space.'

'We were supposed to go abroad together.'

'You have your entire lives to go away together, Milly. While he's away, have some fun with your friends.'

'I will,' I said defiantly. *And punish Mike at the same time.*

'Good – dry your eyes, go home and return tomorrow with a smile. The show must go on.'

That evening Mum said, 'Mike called for the umpteenth time, Milly, and wants you to call him back.'

'I'll never speak to him again,' I snapped, then slammed the living room door and ran upstairs to sob, face down, on my purple candlewick bedspread for the millionth time that week.

I refused to talk to Mike, and the day he left for Valencia, I muttered, 'I hope he chokes on an orange and dies,' as I tidied away a new batch of sleeveless skinny-rib tops in Togs.

'Fancy going out tonight?' said the Saturday girl who was sixteen going on thirty. 'Our local pub, the Coach and Horses, is always hopping on a Saturday.'

'Yes, sure,' I said. 'But we're underage.'

'Slap on the slap and nobody will notice – besides, the landlord is short-sighted and reminds me of Colonel Blink. He thought my nan was a man last week and called her *sir*.'

For the first time in days, I laughed and said, 'Okay, you're on.'

Colonel Blink ('the short-sighted gink') was a cartoon character from *The Beezer*. He was a pompous, ex-military man with a walrus moustache and glasses with milk-bottle-bottom lenses, and his frequent interjection was 'Gad, Sir!'

I donned my shortest mini skirt and tightest skinny-rib jumper, plastered on foundation, powder, black eyeliner and pale pink frosted lipstick, shoved my hair into a beehive. As a finishing touch, I nicked a spray of Mum's Sultry Nights fragrance (I was obsessed by its spicy and warm amber seductiveness) and tottered out in my highest heels.

In the busy pub, a tall and gorgeous blue-eyed blonde man approached our table. In a foreign accent, he said, 'We're going for a meal. Would you like to join us?' He motioned towards his equally cute friend.

Unanimously we said yes and were soon eating delicious Lancashire hotpots in a small but friendly cafe, Flo's of Lodge Lane, along with red wine. For pudding, we had steamed jam sponges drenched with custard, and it was all delicious.

My divine date was polite, not pushy – I was the pushy one. After paying the bill, he said, 'I'll walk you home, Milly.'

I fluttered my fake eyelashes. 'I'd rather you walked me to your place.' I was determined to punish Mike. Besides, this muscled, blonde and beautiful Finnish sailor sent my teenage hormones into overdrive.

A decent and direct chap, he looked me in the eyes. 'It will be a one-night stand as we sail tomorrow, and I have obligations in Finland.'

'One night's enough for me, come on, let's go,' I said brazenly.

Despite him being rather talented in bed (understatement) the moment I awoke in the shabby hotel room, sober, I regretted my rash decision. How would I tell Mike? Dare I ever tell Mike? I couldn't live with the secret. Ashamed, I realised I'd over-reacted to his holiday and was a big fat hypocrite. If I'd been offered a free or cheap holiday abroad, with or without Mike, I'd have gone in a flash. And I'd bite Prill's hand off for an overseas buying trip – but that was work, I reasoned unreasonably.

But I didn't tell Mike because he never came home.

He died when the balcony of a shoddily built hotel crumbled, crashed to the ground and killed Mike and his mates, who were drinking beer and eating paella on the terrace – they were the only casualties.

My intense guilt and grief were horrendous, I sleepwalked through life and work, and it was a miracle Prill didn't sack me.

Then I discovered I was pregnant.

And the baby wasn't Mike's – my diary said so.

What a mess.

I didn't want an abortion but told Mum I was pregnant, the baby was Mike's, and I wanted it adopted the moment it was born – and didn't want to see it.

Mum, in choked tones, said, 'Keep your baby, and we'll manage, darling – we always do.'

'No – I never want to see it,' I repeated. 'Mike shouldn't have gone on holiday without me.'

'But you loved each other, Milly. It was just a silly tiff.'

To give Mum a reason for the adoption, I lied and said, 'I hate Mike and never loved him.'

I love him so much and always will. How could I have betrayed him? I can't keep this baby who'll forever remind me of my guilt and shame. Oh, I hate myself and want to die.

Hugging me, Mum said, 'I know you're lying, Milly – you and Mike adored each other.'

Her soft, understanding tone broke me, and I told her everything.

We devised a convoluted plan, made easier because Mike was an orphan who'd lived with his ancient great-grandma I'd never met.

'I can guess much of this plan,' said Prill now. 'You arranged to have the baby adopted then told everyone, including me, that it died.'

'Yes,' I muttered. 'I didn't know what else to do but have always felt guilty. When it was born, I covered my eyes until the midwife took it away. I didn't even know if it was a boy or a girl.' It was the only way to stay sane (ish).

'So you never saw your baby?'

'No – I'm so ashamed, and it's an awful secret I've carried for years. Even my first husband didn't know.'

'Didn't know you'd been pregnant?'

'He knew that – but I told everyone the same story about the baby dying.'

Years of guilt and regret bubbled to the surface, and I sobbed my heart out.

'You're too hard on yourself, darling. Sadly, millions of women have had babies adopted for various reasons. As the saying goes, *Don't judge a person unless you've walked in their shoes.*'

'I suppose.'

After a dramatic pause, Prill said, 'Anyway, you now have the chance to make amends ... Tuppence is your daughter.'

Every nerve in my body prickled.

Tuppence? That gorgeous young woman with the beautiful big blue eyes?

Deep in my heart, I'd always known my baby was loved and cared for, but this was time to make amends for giving her away.

'There's something else,' said Prill.

'About Tuppence?' My tummy churned as I awaited more trouble.

'Yes – she's a witch.'

Talk about the universe having a dark sense of humour.

It was too much, and I crumpled to the floor in a sobbing heap. As a blubbering wreck, I was useless to Tuppence and might fail her a second time.

But Prill threw some silver dust at me and incanted a spell. 'This is no time for overt emotion; pragmatically, you must find a solution.'

Instantly, my mind regained a modicum of calm and logic.

'Feeling better, Milly?' said Prill.

'Yes.'

'I'm not surprised – I sprinkled you with calm and coherence dust, and although time is still of the essence, level-headedness is more important than speed. The correct methods to unravel this mystery will come quicker if we stay calm and act naturally. Nor must we lose our sense of humour as it elevates us above evil – gives us a running start.'

'How do you mean?'

'The more spiritual a person, the more playful – they understand that life is a game. The nastier someone is deep in their soul, the more miserable they appear to others unless they possess the Wolf in Sheep's Clothing spell. A calm attitude while solving Tuppence's situation will put us steps ahead of those with evil intent.'

'What's the Wolf in Sheep's Clothing Spell?'

'A terrible spell which makes an evil person appear altruistic and convivial to all.'

I shuddered. 'That sounds awful.'

'It is – and very dangerous in the wrong hands. How do you feel now, Milly?'

After a scan of my inner being, I said, 'My maternal hysteria has somewhat faded, replaced with determination.'

Saphira, who'd been unusually quiet, put a comforting paw on my arm, and it touched and comforted me immensely, more than any words.

It was weird that witches surrounded me, yet I wasn't one, nor was Fawn, although her mum, head of the WFGC – the Witches For Good Council, was a powerful witch. It was she who decided where, when and how to spend magic spells.

From books and films, I'd thought witches used magic willy-nilly. Like Samantha Stevens from *Bewitched* – stopped only by Darrin – or Derwood as the marvellous Endora called him. In reality, spells use lots of energy, and each witch and warlock has an allotted amount each month, with a small allocation for personal use – rather like pocket money.

Not surprisingly, I couldn't stop thinking of Tuppence and said, 'If Tuppence is a witch, how did Simon manipulate her so easily?'

Prill said, 'Tuppence originally manipulated Simon to stop him from becoming like Reggie Ratchet as he was destined to do in the future.'

'Who's he?'

She wrinkled her nose as if she'd smelt rotten fish. 'An unpleasant landlord who exploited the London post-war housing shortage. In the 1950s, he bought run-down buildings in Paddington, evicted the sitting tenants, then relet the properties at exorbitant prices. To maximise profits, he got rid of sitting tenants by means most foul.'

'What sort of means most foul?' I said.

'Refused to install jacuzzis,' Saphira cackled.

'It's not funny, Saphira,' scolded Prill. 'He deliberately drove the sitting tenants crazy with all-night parties and loud music in neighbouring rooms.'

'Sounds like most buildings in London,' I said.

Saphira sniggered.

Prill pursed her lips, trying not to laugh. 'You two are a match made in hell. Anyway, if the loud noise tactics didn't work, Reggie Ratchet sent henchmen to cut off electricity, break locks and smash toilets.'

'Did he improve the buildings when he got higher rents?' I said.

'Hardly at all, apart from the bare minimum.'

'How did he get away with it?'

'The new tenants were usually immigrant families with nowhere else to go. While his tenants lived in squalor, Reggie Ratchet was in a decadent four-storey house in London's Knightsbridge, and a chauffeur drove him around in a blue Rolls Royce.

'I hope he got his comeuppance,' I said. 'You should have set Saphira onto him.'

'I didn't know her or Rachet then,' said Prill.

'I'd have scratched his eyes out.' Saphira sharpened her claws on a sofa.

'Oy, Saphira – lay off our new furniture,' I scolded.

'Sorry – primitive cat instincts – I'd have killed Ratchet with sarcasm had I known.'

'You usually call it sarcatm, Saphira.'

'That too – it's deadlier.'

Curious, I urged Prill to continue. 'Did Reggie Ratchet get away with it?'

'No – he enjoyed strong coffee, and someone with a grudge added poison to the brew, and he dropped dead. At first, the police believed it was a heart attack, but it turned out the "heart attack" was caused by a lethal dose of succitupamine, and Ratchet died within seconds of his last earthly sip of coffee.'

This story was a tad familiar.

'Succitupamine? Is that a joke name?' I said.

'No – it's a bitter-tasting poison which emulates a fatal heart attack.'

'Prill, can you look into the crystal ball and see who murdered Simon?' I said.

'I'll try, but I doubt it – you know how temperamental it is.'

Heart in mouth, I watched Prill gaze into the globe as she groaned.

'What's up?'

'Tuppence's witch magic is fading fast.'

'Why?'

'She has a fresh vampire aura.'

Despite the calm and coherence spell, the love I'd buried for my first child flooded me in a tsunami of emotion, and I knew I must rescue her from both a murder charge and vampirism. 'Tuppence is a fresh vampire? What does that mean?'

'Someone bit her recently.'

With a shudder, I recalled the marks on her neck. 'So even if we rescue her, she'll be a vampire?'

Prill smiled soothingly. 'If we prove her innocence in time, I'll administer the vampire-reversal spell, which works on fresh vampires.'

'Why have we got to prove her innocence first? Can't you incant the spell now?'

Prill shook her head sadly. 'No.'

'Why?'

'It's complicated – but in short, she must be within five yards of my presence within minutes of midnight on Halloween when I administer the spell. And I must also be in no doubt of her innocence.'

My heart fell. 'That's a tiny window of opportunity – it's Halloween this Saturday. What if we don't succeed?'

In sympathetic tones, Prill said, 'Tuppence would not survive without consuming blood, and the idea, even as a vampire, might horrify her, and she'd starve to death.'

'Why might consuming blood horrify a vampire?'

'Tuppence has a sweet soul.'

I remembered her Finnish dad – sweet and unassuming – but he'd obviously had magical connections. A horrible thought struck me in the solar plexus. What if I couldn't prove Tuppence's innocence, and she became a full vampire. 'How could my daughter get blood in prison, Prill?' I said.

'Use your imagination, darling – many prisons are violent places.'

'How is she surviving without blood now?'

'Fresh vampires can consume regular food for the first few months.'

It was undoubtedly food – or blood – for thought.

'But what if...'

Prill held up her hand. 'Our minds need to relax now – we'll make a fresh start tomorrow. Pop the television on, Milly.'

Love at First Bite was on BBC1 – ironic.

'Shall I change channels?' I said.

Prill shook her head. 'No – this film is fun. And a bit of trivia – the makeup artist, William Tuttle, did the makeup for the 1931 Dracula movie with Bela Lugosi.'

'He must be getting on,' I said.

'Cheek – he's only seventy-five – a similar age to me when I died.'

When Dracula (George Hamilton) and his girlfriend (Susan Saint James) took to the dancefloor, we watched raptly. As Prill and I tapped our toes and jiggled on the sofa, Saphira leapt to the floor and shimmied around on her hind legs to 'I Love the Nightlife'.

Despite my motherly concern, the silly film took my mind off worries a little – and showed me that perhaps vampires weren't all bad.

When the film finished, Prill gave me a stern look. 'Hard as it may be, Milly, go about life as usual from tomorrow – clues are more likely to appear if you trust the universe, go with the flow. Don't run around questioning everyone blindly, although I doubt you could under the calm and coherence spell. Meanwhile, Saphira and I will do what we can in the background. Now, get some sleep as I wish to chat with Saphira.'

That was me dismissed from my living room, but I trusted Prill and said, 'Goodnight, Prill and Saphira.'

'Goodnight,' they chorused, and Saphira, nestled on Prill's lap, waved a paw.

In bed later, Robbie was too drunk to talk and fell into a coma minutes after his head hit the feather pillows. As he and Saphira snored, I thought of Tuppence and mulled over the scary situation. Priority was to find Simon's actual killer before Halloween so Prill could reverse my daughter's vampirism.

And Halloween was imminent.

Also, we must unearth the other vampires and neutralise their dark power – perhaps administer the reversal spell to any fresh vampires.

A doddle – we should manage that in a few hours. Not.

Prill had said there were ways to destroy full vampires without driving stakes through their hearts.

There'd better be, I thought as sleep eluded me, as I wanted to murder the vampire who'd bitten Tuppence. What if she became a full vampire? Despite the magic dust, the idea was too awful to contemplate.

Also, Prill had said that crucifixes and garlic were useless vampire deterrents effective only in fiction. And that Fawn and I should take over Rich and Pour and distribute the magic shortbread to help assuage vampire or other dark energy vibes.

Sleep further evaded me as I remembered the sad days in the private mother and baby home – where I gave birth with the help of a lovely midwife – and they took my baby away, handed it to the adoptive parents – all with my agreement. However, the staff thoroughly vetted the prospective parents beforehand. Mum, the best judge of character I know, met them at my insistence, and she said they were a kind-hearted couple.

Another teenager, Connie, distraught at giving away her son, pushed into it by a strict mother, begged me to see my baby. 'Spend time with it before the adoptive parents arrive, Milly.'

'Thanks – but I can't face it.' Because the floodgates would have opened and never stopped – so I buried my guilt and grief deep – to eat away at me for years.

I'll never forget Connie's screams when they took her baby son from her loving arms. And the guilt when I hadn't even held or looked at my baby – but I didn't dare. However, I'd done something I deeply regretted and now had a chance to make amends.

Blood from a Vampire

29th October 1987

I awoke to loud protestations from Robbie. 'Why did I do it, Milly? Oh, my head. Remind me never to go out with Terry again.'

'Shall I get you an aspirin or ten?' I said.

'Yes, please, industrial strength – and strong coffee.' He peeked his head from under the duvet as his breath emitted a vile stench of stale onion, garlic and alcohol, and I quickly quit the hazardous area.

Padding through the living room to the kitchen, I greeted Saphira, who was wide awake on the sofa. 'Good morning, your majesty. Up so soon?'

'Yes – I was awakened at 3 am by a hideous odour emanating from Robbie. It smelt worse than the vilest cat litter ever.'

What would you know about cat litter, Saphira? You use human loos.'

I'd once inadvertently spotted her through a part-open bathroom door when she perched delicately on the toilet seat and even flushed afterwards.

'I know about cat litter from when I was undercover.'

'Undercover? When?'

56

'When Prill ran Baking and Entering, she suspected a female staff member – Doris – of theft. Doris took a shine to me, and I pretended to like her and visited her horrid home many times.'

I smiled. 'That sounds like you rang the front doorbell.'

'Don't be silly – I entered through open windows or doors like any self-respecting feline. If everything was closed, I magically appeared.'

'Did Doris have a family?'

'Yes, her husband was as horrid as she was, but the young son was a sweet black-haired angel. I couldn't believe he'd sprung from their loins.'

My tummy heaved at the latter. 'That's a vision I didn't need, Saphira. Did they have any pets?'

'Yes – an ugly tomcat whose rancid litter was rarely changed.'

'And? Tell me about your undercover activities.'

'Well, it was hideously boring. For many evenings, I sat in a drab lounge with dreary Doris and her boring husband. The latter wore a dirty string vest and scratched his unmentionables as they watched awful programmes on television or indulged in inane chatter. Finally, the husband said, "How much did you nick from the old bag's till this week, Doris?" and she replied, "Sixty quid". I was livid.'

Outraged on Prill's behalf, I said, 'How horrid.'

'Exactly. I was angry, more about dreary Doris calling fab Prill an old bag – she was only in her sixties at the time and in better shape than most forty-year-olds.'

'What did you do?'

Saphira buried her head in her front paws. 'I'm ashamed to say.'

Now I was dying to know. 'What?'

'I immobilised them with a spell and used the open box of chocolates on the coffee table as a cat litter.'

I clapped a hand to my mouth. 'You never did!'

'Yes – I then said, "If you steal again, Doris, I'll make a cat litter of both your lives. And if you or your husband ever discuss this incident with anyone, I'll turn you into newts." Luckily, their nice son was out that evening, but I terrified his parents.'

'Was that slight overkill, Saphira?' I said.

'Absolutely not. At close range to Mr and Mrs Rascal, my extra-sensory cat perception went into overdrive, and I knew they would cause much misery to many if I didn't stop them in their nasty tracks. So I put the fear of Bastet into them.'

'Bastet?'

'The Goddess of cats.'

'I thought that was you.'

Saphira laughed as Robbie staggered into the room, bleary-eyed, and she wrinkled her nose and made a swift exit.

'Can you run me into Brighton, Milly?' he said. 'I'm supposed to meet Terry at 9 am.'

I told him to grab a painkiller from the kitchen cabinet, zoomed upstairs, and we were soon trundling into Brighton.

I eyed the dark sky and said, 'I hope storms aren't imminent.'

Robbie turned on the car radio as Michael Salmon, the respected weather-forecast man, said, 'Ten minutes ago, a local farmer rang, saying a hurricane will wreak havoc across southern England at the weekend. But rest assured, because I forecast calm and clement weather.'

'You don't think there'll be a hurricane, do you, Robbie?' I said.

'Nah! Michael Salmon hasn't got it wrong yet. He said our wedding day would be gorgeous, and it was, in every way.' He squeezed my thigh as my eyes filled with happy tears.

'Where are you meeting Terry?' I asked as we walked through busy Brighton Lanes hand-in-hand.

'Didn't I say?'

'Not that I recall.'

'Rich and Pour.'

'Mind if I come with?'

'Not at all, but...'

He hesitated.

I twigged. 'Ah, you want to be alone.'

'Sort of – at our own table, at least.'

'Tell you what, if there's no spare table in Rich and Pour, I'll check out my future competition – Sweetie Pie.'

'You'll hate the place – it's stuffy.'

'Then why do you go there?'

'I have my reasons, but it's partly to schmooze for customers.'

Tempted to pry further, I gave Robbie his space. If he preferred Sweetie Pie for morning coffee over Rich and Pour, what business was it of mine?

One thing I learned in my former stifling marriage was I need relationship space. I might have got offended when Steve (first husband) wanted me out of the way, but now I respected and loved Robbie's occasional need for privacy. And he mine, I hoped – or perhaps he thought me a battle-axe.

As we reached Rich and Pour, Terry waved from a window table, and the place was heaving. So I pecked Robbie on the lips and headed to Sweetie Pie.

As I walked into a starched, fun-free atmosphere, bare walls painted white to match the marble floor, then sat on a stylish but uncomfortable chair, a po-faced haughty woman, probably the proprietor, said, 'You should wait to be seated.'

'Sorry – shall I move?'

'No, you may stay there,' she said begrudgingly.

'Thanks.'

I studied the menu, and the prices were twice Rich and Pour's, and there was no Cheesy Chip Mountain available. It was table service, and a snooty waitress with a starched apron and starchier attitude took my order for eggs benedict and coffee.

Did they get their staff from Snobs R Us?

While I waited in the frigid atmosphere, 'enjoying' the dirge-like background music and the acrid scent of burnt toast, Tallon and William arrived and sat at the only spare table in a dark corner. Why was this joyless place busy? It had the happy atmosphere of school detention, and I almost pulled the small Silvine notebook from my handbag to write *I must not enjoy myself* fifty times.

And the surrounding conversations, in hushed, reverent tones, were all about trust funds, investments and getting children into 'the right school'. Three portly men in pinstripe suits banged on about profit, loss and equities as they banged numbers into calculators in between scoffing scones and slurping tea.

Something about the pinstriped trio's vibe gave me the creeps. It was as if they'd sold their souls to the devil, and I shook my head to dispel the horrid thought. *Get a grip, Milly – perhaps it's your imagination.*

So I caught the eye of the fattest of the three, smiled, and he gave a death-ray glare as my tummy clenched with fear.

Halfway through my awful breakfast – the eggs were bullets, the hollandaise sauce lumpy, the coffee weak, Tallon stormed out as William sobbed into his tomato juice.

I hastened over to the poor lad. 'May I join you?'

'Please do,' he sniffed.

I sat beside him. 'What's up?'

'I left a tap on in Books and Bites last night, and the carpet is drenched. Tallon is furious.'

'Could someone else have left it on?' I said.

His eyes brightened as if surprised someone had faith in him and didn't automatically assume he was the culprit. 'That's just it,' he said. 'I have slight OCD, well pretty bad OCD actually, and I always check at least five times.'

'Were you last in Books and Bites before the flood?'

'Yes. But you make it sound like Noah's ark – it wasn't that bad, but Tallon has a terrible temper.'

'Does anyone else have a key?'

'Only Tallon.'

'Have you had new keys cut recently?' *Gosh – my suspicious mind.* Or perhaps the calm and coherence spell was working.

'Why, yes – the other day.'

'Where?' I said.

'In the nearby department store on the ground floor.'

'You mean Henderson's?' This was Tarquin's store.

'Yes.'

It was like getting blood from a stone – or vampire.

'How long did you leave the master key with them?'

'Overnight. I used Tallon's key meanwhile.'

'Ah, so many people could have accessed the original?'

He clasped his hands as if in prayer. 'Oh, I hope you're right. Why didn't I think of that?'

'It's often hard to think when we're upset.'

'Tell me about it.'

Who would wish to sabotage Books and Bites? Or was it simply carelessness?

When the poor man, or poor vampire, burst into tears, I handed him a tissue from my handbag, and as he dried his eyes, I said, 'Is it just the flooded premises you're upset about.'

He grimaced. 'No – Tallon said the new carpet must come from my wages – a fiver a week – so I'll be in debt for years.'

'Were any books damaged?'

'None or I'd be suicidal. I hate running the cafe but love the books. I wish it were just called Books, not Books and Bites.'

Teasing him, and possibly on shaky ground, I said, 'What have you got against bites?'

'I can't say.'

'You can tell me everything.'

He stared into my eyes as darkness fought light, and light won. 'It's odd, but I feel I *can* tell you everything – there's something about you. I haven't confided in anyone in centuries.'

'Centuries?'

He waved a beringed hand. 'Oh, I mean ages – I often exaggerate, like when someone says they are prehistoric instead of old or they've had an item of clothing for yonks, or whatever.'

Methinks he doth protest too much. I had an open and friendly vampire to quiz and didn't intend to lose my chance. 'Talk to me.'

But opportunity closed along with his expression, which went from open to shut. Then I remembered I had a foil-wrapped piece of magic shortbread in my bag and hoped he was one of those vampires who could consume other things apart from blood – and tomato juice. Because the magic shortbread also encouraged people to be open and truthful.

'I'm still a bit peckish,' I said. 'Can I get you anything?'

'I'd love another tomato juice and a slice of peach pie with vanilla ice cream, thanks.'

Great – that confirmed he could eat. And perhaps he didn't drink blood – just tomato juice, conveniently the same colour.

As I spotted shortbread biscuits on the counter, a dastardly plan formed. I beckoned the starchy waitress and said, 'May we please have a cappuccino, a tomato juice, a shortbread biscuit and a slice of peach pie with vanilla ice cream?'

'Surely.' She eyed my unfinished breakfast suspiciously. 'Was anything wrong with your eggs benedict?' her mouth said as her eyes said, 'Say yes, and I'll murder you.'

Everything. 'No, but I'm craving something sweet.'

When she delivered the goods, I awaited an opportune moment to enact my plan.

Luckily, William said, 'I feel a little faint, so I'll add my iron supplement to this tomato juice.' He ferreted around in his purple handbag and pulled out a small vial, and emptied its contents into his drink, and I was confident it was blood. He stirred it like some older people stir tea (endlessly until it goes cold and with as much noise as possible).

I surreptitiously broke Sweetie Pie's shortbread into three and did the same with the shortbread from my handbag, careful to separate the types.

Taking a bite of Sweetie Pie's shortbread, I moaned as if having an orgasm – definitely fake as it was sawdust compared to mine and Saphira's ambrosial delights.

'Whatever's in that, I want some,' said William.

I handed him a chunk of magic shortbread and waited as he popped it in his mouth.

His eyes rolled upwards, and he moaned with delight. If the magic worked on vampires, he would soon feel positive and be unable to fib for at least half an hour.

'That was the best shortbread I've ever tasted,' he said. 'And I'm suddenly happy, less scared of Tallon than in ages.'

'Are you usually scared of him?'

'Terrified, but now I want to tell him where to shove his rigid rules.'

As he rose, I put a gentle restraining hand on his arm. 'Not now. Come to my house tonight, and we'll discuss how to handle Tallon.'

His eyes gleamed with hope. 'I'm almost scared to come as I'm desperate to tell you secret stuff, but excited because I know you won't use it against me. I hope I'm not delusional.'

'You're not. So you'll come?'

'Try to stop me. What time?'

'8 pm.' As insurance, I added, 'And guess what?'

'What?'

'I made that shortbread biscuit.'

He frowned. 'But you just ordered it.'

'Yes, but I had another in my bag.'

Eyes narrowed, he surveyed me suspiciously.

I handed over two bits of shortbread. 'Try this, then the other,' indicating William should try Sweetie Pie's vile version first.

He spat it into his napkin.

'Ew, that's horrible,' he said as the snooty waitress glared.

After confirming arrangements, I grabbed my bag as a sobbing, handcuffed Tuppence passed by outside, escorted by two burly police officers.

And my motherly heart broke.

Sleuths

I rose to pursue her, but William said, 'Don't get involved, or you might make things worse. I've spent months regretting something I did in the heat of the moment.'

He sounded less effeminate, and I suspected his flippant attitude was a cover for something more profound. It was time to make enquiries, and I wished Fawn were here to assist.

As I walked along Brighton Lanes, wondering where to start, I craved a decent cup of coffee to help me think and went in search of Brighton's best.

To my amazement, Fawn was behind Rich and Pour's counter, frothing milk.

With a shriek, she ran into my arms. 'Oh, I'm so glad to see you.'

Rita said, 'Take her away, Milly – she's driving me nuts, and I want to enjoy my last few days here.'

'But I was making a cappuccino,' said Fawn.

Rita narrowed her eyes. 'Sit down, and I'll bring it over. Do you want one, Milly?'

'Please, Rita.'

Fawn rubbed her flat tummy. 'I'm starving.'

Knowing she'd be no help without food, I suggested the Cheesy Chip Mountain.

She gasped. 'That sounds amazing. Shall we have one each, Milly?'

'One portion between us is fine – you'll eat most of it anyway and, as usual, won't gain an ounce.'

Fawn lived up to her name with her Bambi-like features and long, slim legs, and I was envious of her 26-year-old metabolism.

Ensconced at a corner table, Fawn began, 'After the Similan Islands, we visited Chiang Mai and rode el...'

I put a hand over hers. 'Tell me later, Fawn, but there's been another murder and other developments, and I need your help.'

'You're joking.'

'Wish I was.' I told her about Tuppence, Tallon, William et al. as her mouth opened wider and wider.

'Oh, my God – Tuppence is your daughter? How are you so calm?'

I told her about the calm and coherence spell. '...And Prill said to act naturally, let fate lead the way as rushing around like a headless chicken achieves nothing.'

Never slow on the uptake, Fawn said, 'Okay, you make enquiries however you see fit. After I've eaten, as I'm faint from hunger, I'll begin with Henderson's key-cutting department.'

'That's what I thought. The staff hardly know me but already love you.'

'Love me. Why?'

'When I visited the Lancôme counter to buy mascara, the consultant sang your praises. Said Tarquin's previous girlfriends often lorded it over the staff, and you're a breath of fresh air.'

Fawn stifled a yawn. 'Oh, that's nice of them, but I'm so jet-lagged. Once I've nipped into Henderson's, I'm off home to sleep. But, I'll quiz Tarquin later – see if he can shed any light.'

'Don't tell him about the vampires, ghosts and stuff – or that I'm Tuppence's mum.'

'Of course not, and he has no clue Mum is a witch. I'll simply discover what I can.'

She hoovered the Cheesy Chip Mountain, air-kissed me, then sped away as fast as jet lag allowed.

I wanted to visit Tuppence, but intuition said to stay away from the police station or wherever she was. Besides, the idea of my daughter in a cell made me nauseous.

Instead, I hastened to Robbie's shop, told him about Tuppence and the police officers, but omitted to mention she was my daughter – that could wait for an opportune moment, and I didn't wish to waste valuable sleuth time on explanations and possible recriminations.

'Oh, that poor girl, but I might have relevant news,' he said.

'What about?'

'Simon's aunt was in earlier, said he was a pussycat a few months back, and she watched him change, start bullying Tuppence, said it was like the devil possessed him.'

'Did this aunt mention what Simon was like before he met Tuppence?'

'Funnily enough, yes. She said he was pleasant but serious, and Tuppence lightened him up. Also said she'd eat her most hated dish – cold rice pudding – if Tuppence had murdered him.'

Good – I knew my daughter couldn't be a murderer. 'Anything else?'

He paused for a moment. 'Don't think so – oh, hang on; she said the man who runs Transylvanian Trinkets seems scary.'

No flies on her. 'Tallon terrifies me, too.'

And I rather fancy him – but will never admit it. Stop it, Milly; your hormones got you into a mess years ago – control them this time.

I remembered William was due at our house that evening. With the questions I wanted to ask, it would be best if Robbie were out. I hated deceiving my husband and wished I could tell him about his ghostly and magical parents. Perhaps it was time to summon Prill and ask her permission, but meanwhile, I had other problems.

About to broach the subject of evicting Robbie for the evening, fate preempted me when he said, 'Erm, do you mind if I meet Terry again tonight, Milly?'

I couldn't sound too enthusiastic, so I injected a little hurt into my voice. *Eat your heart out, Meryl Streep.* 'Terry. Again. Why?'

'His mate wants me to source a Bentley Continental.'

'So, it's business?'

'Of course. I wouldn't leave you two nights in a row for pure pleasure. You're pleasure enough for me.'

He winked, *Carry On* style, and I giggled then said, 'Fawn's back.'

'Good – you two are great together. I'm glad you're taking over Rich and Pour.'

'Me too.'

But why did I have nagging doubts? It was strange, but I fancied working in Books and Bites with William, although I should be scared that he was a vampire. But he seemed sweet, and the idea of working in a bookshop was heaven.

In London, Fawn had suggested making Scone but Not Forgotten into a book cafe, but I wasn't ready for it, probably as I knew nothing about running cafes and was nervous. But dealing with murder, ghosts, witches, and vampires put worry about everyday tasks into the shade and, besides, the London cafe had gone well, and I was now more confident.

I happily imagined combining my two great loves (apart from Robbie) into one – books and baking. However, I preferred the eating of the baking more than the making of the baking.

At home, early evening, Robbie said, 'What will you do tonight, Milly?'

'William's popping over.'

'Maybe I should stay in.'

I laughed. 'You're not usually jealous. Anyway, relax – he's as camp as a row of tents.'

He pressed a palm to his heart theatrically. 'Thank God for that, or I would just die.'

Robbie

After Milly and I kissed goodbye, I drove into Brighton.

When I parked my car in Terry's sweeping drive, he appeared and said, 'Hi, Robbie. There's a change of plan because I got some lamb.'

He was a poet and didn't know it. 'What do you mean?'

'I'd planned a bottle of champers in the Ship Hotel, then the Ashoka

for curry and a bottle or three of red, but I spotted a lovely leg of lamb in the butcher's window and bought it.'

'Are you cooking it?'

'Of course not – that's Audrey's job.'

'You said she was seeing *Wish You Were Here* in the Savoy Cinema with a friend.'

'Yes, but she's a stay-at-home wife, and my needs come first.'

What a charmer – he thought he was living in the 1950s or the dark ages.

After Terry led me into a spacious kitchen with a large central black granite island, he gestured to a squashy blue sofa. 'Park your bum while I grab the bubbly. Damnation – Audrey was supposed to put out nibbles.' Then he screamed at the top of his voice, so my eardrums nearly burst, 'Audrey, where are the nuts and crisps and stuff?'

If I spoke, or shouted, to Milly like that, she'd leave me and with good reason.

Audrey came through the back door laden with Posh Nosh carrier bags.

'Did you get mint sauce and redcurrant jelly as I told you?' said Terry.

'Yes, and everything else on your long list. It's not fair – you're supposed to be out, and I was supposed to see *Witches of Eastwick* with Sue.'

Eyes narrowed, Terry said, 'You said *Wish You Were Here.*'

'Er, the tickets sold out.'

'Good – because I'll see *Witches of Eastwick* with you – that Susan Sarandon is a bit of alright, as are Cher and Michelle Pfeiffer – cor!'

He gave a Sid James chuckle as Audrey said in a strained tone, 'And Jack Nicholson is a *bit of alright* as you so charmingly put it, *darling*, so we'll be quits.'

Terry folded his arms. 'A bit of politeness wouldn't go amiss, Audrey, as we have a guest.'

Appalled at Terry's manner, I wanted to defend Audrey but worried it could make things worse, so I followed a neutral path and said nothing.

'We'll go through to the living room while you get started. How long until dinner, Audrey?' said Terry.

'About an hour and a half, an hour if you're happy with pink.'

Terry caught my eye. 'Do you like your meat rare like a man?'

No, I hate it like that. 'Erm, yes, of course.' I didn't wish to add more hassle to Audrey's spoiled evening.

The living room reflected Terry's brashness rather than Audrey's elegance – it was crowded with a mishmash of colours, styles, and eras – from Victorian to Art Deco to Habitat.

We spent an hour talking about cars, always a pleasure, before a gong rang. A gong? What was this? A hotel? Terry seemed to think so.

I imagined myself without the family jewels if I spoke to Milly the way Terry addressed Audrey. How did men get away with it? Why did women put up with it? And it was sometimes the other way round. Behind closed doors, Dad's best friend had been constantly bullied by his wife, who seemed a meek-mannered soul in public.

At her funeral, Dad asked his friend how he felt, and he said, 'Like I've been reborn.'

I felt reborn with my darling Milly and knew how lucky I was.

If only Mum had lived long enough to see us married. And Dad, for that matter. I didn't fully appreciate them while they were alive, and I'd give anything to see them again. I'd led them a merry dance with my gambling and other problems and wished I could start again. Although I was happy with Milly, this was my sadness and regret.

Audrey popped her elegant head through the door. 'Terry, your mum's on the phone.'

He gave an exasperated sigh and left the room as Audrey said, 'May I join you for a few moments, Robbie? Dinner is in the hostess trolley.'

'Be my guest; it's your house.'

'You wouldn't think so, would you? I'm so embarrassed by how Terry treats me.'

'He's the one who should be embarrassed, but I must admit I'm rather shocked.'

'Ah, yes, because of the contrast of Mr Bonhomie outside the house and Mr Bully inside the house. But it's odd as most never see his dark side, and he enjoys gaslighting me, says I'm paranoid, and he's a pussycat. Oh, look, a rerun of one of my favourite shows just started – *My Mother the Car*.' She nodded towards the television.

'I remember it from the 1960s,' I said. It's about a man whose dead mum reincarnates as a 1928 Porter and communicates with him through the car's radio. I loved it.

'Would you be scared if your mum haunted your car?' said Audrey.

'No – I'd love Mum back in any shape or form.' I dug my fingernails into my palms to stop the tears – too embarrassing – and then recognised a familiar fragrance and sniffed appreciatively.

'Dinner will be ready soon.' Audrey obviously mistook my large sniff for impatience to eat.

'Dinner smells good, but I also just got a whiff of my mother's favourite perfume – Arpege.'

'That's my favourite, too,' said Audrey.

'Are you wearing it now?'

'Yes.'

'I thought so.'

Not Mum haunting me, then – I was disappointed.

Terry blustered into the room and said, 'Back to the kitchen with you, Audrey. The men have a car to discuss.'

It was difficult not to slug him, but I wanted the money for the Aston Martin. Terry knew his antiques, but I was more knowledgeable about cars than most. Worryingly I was becoming more grasping and devious and had not been entirely honest about the car's condition because I suspected the head gasket was faulty but hadn't mentioned it.

Strangely my avarice escalated whenever I ate Sweetie Pie's apple pie, now a morning ritual I rarely resisted. But it left a bad taste in my mouth, which I often counteracted with a piece of Milly's shortbread snaffled from our kitchen.

Dinner was delicious, and Audrey must have seen my horror at the idea of bloody meat, had pan-seared my portion, and it was moreish and the roast potatoes perfect.

'What have you done to the potatoes? Milly's and mine never turn out great,' I said.

'I parboil them, drain them, salt them, then pop the lid on the pan, shake it all about, then put them in searing hot fat.'

'It's not the flipping Hokey Cokey,' said Terry, and we all laughed.

After that, Terry was convivial to Audrey, and it turned into a pleasant evening.

After vintage port and ripe Stilton, I was pie-eyed, so Terry suggested staying the night.

'Oh, do,' enthused Audrey. 'We have spare toothbrushes, and you can borrow a pair of Terry's pyjamas. And the spare-room bed is bliss – it's a newish mattress, and I often sleep in there.'

Terry cast a warning look. 'Don't give visitors the wrong impression. We hardly ever sleep separately.' His eyes twinkled naughtily. 'Audrey can't bear to be separated from me, can you, darling?'

Unnoticed by Terry, she gritted her teeth. 'No, darling, can't resist your manly charms.'

The arrogant git seemed unaware of the sarcasm.

Before I got into bed, I laughed at myself in the mirror – Terry's pyjama bottoms ended four inches above my ankles.

Short men were so often bullies.

An Evening with William

After Robbie and I kissed goodbye, I decided to change into something evening-like. What to wear? A Morticia-Addams-style outfit, perhaps. *Don't be silly, Milly.* I compromised with a black velour tracksuit with a diamante neckline and huge shoulder pads. Crazily, shoulder pads were getting bigger and bigger – surely the craze must end soon?

In the living room, I burst out laughing. Saphira was in a black cloak, and her eye teeth were longer and fanglike.

'What are you up to, you daft cat?' I said.

'I'm on my guard as William's a vampire.'

'Are vampire cats a thing?'

'Of course – they even have mini vampire coffins.' She waved a paw as eerie theremin music permeated the room, and a feline-sized black coffin floated from the ceiling.

Vampire bats fluttered in my tummy. 'Saphira, be a normal cat tonight or at least look normal.'

'Normal is overrated – pah.'

But she turned clockwise three times, and the cloak and scary fangs disappeared. Thank God.

At the designated time, William arrived, dapper in a purple velvet jacket, tight black jeans, and a frilly red shirt, emanating a mysteriously dark, musky fragrance with a hint of red roses.

'What's that gorgeous aftershave?' I said.

He giggled. 'It's Vixen – the new perfume advertised on telly.'

'It's divine.'

Note to self – buy some.

'Oh, I love this room,' William squealed.

'Thanks, so do I.' The new decor of green and red with floral chintz made it cosier than its former pastel incarnation. 'Take a seat and help yourself to nibbles.'

But not on my neck.

On the large oak coffee table was an array of snacks – cheese and onion crisps, cashew nuts, sausage rolls, olives, and mushroom pate on melba toast. William nibbled a sausage roll dipped in mustard, then requested tomato juice. I fetched some from the fridge and wondered if he'd add his 'health supplement'.

He did.

Bravely I said. 'That looks interesting. Is it from Nuts About Health on Western Road?'

'Erm no, – a specialist shop in London. You won't have heard of it.'

I'd heard of blood banks alright but wasn't saying that.

After his fix, William said, 'I don't suppose you have more of that gorgeous shortbread?'

'Under that cloth.' I gestured to a covered plate.

He obviously wanted to wolf down the biscuits, but I sensed polite restraint as he nibbled.

Saphira had said William must have good in his soul, or the magic shortbread would be ineffective, albeit tasty.

I knew this was true from the previous murder in London when the victim was a vile man and the only person whose mood hadn't elevated via the magic shortbread.

After William swallowed the last crumbs of the first biscuit, his face unclouded, his scary paleness became a light-pink hue, his lips appeared less blue.

'How's it going with Tallon?' I asked, then wished I hadn't as William's face turned snowy white.

The poor lad shuddered. 'He's furious about the flood, and I can't cope with his awful anger.'

Sad for the poor young man, I offered him another shortbread biscuit.

As he munched, his face cleared again. 'Can I tell you something?'

'Of course.'

'This is the happiest I've been in ages, but don't tell Tallon, or he'll kill me.'

'Oh, I'm sure he's not that bad,' I lied.

'You have no idea. Where's the little girls' room? I must powder my nose.'

'The red door in the hall.'

When he exited stage left, the phone rang – and I crossed the spacious room to answer it.

Fawn.

'I have news,' she gasped.

'Yes?'

'I sleuthed in Henderson's today after I bought a few goodies from the perfumery department.'

'You must own an entire shop by now. Punters should bypass Henderson's and come straight to your bedroom.'

'Dressing room, darling. It's huge. Pop over tomorrow morning, I'll show you around the stately pile, and then we'll scheme.'

'About what?'

'Don't be obtuse – how to solve the murder, thwart the vampires and plan our new business.'

'Great, that's tomorrow, but I have a guest and mustn't neglect him. Meanwhile, what's the main news from your sleuthing, Fawn?'

'Jimmy Ratchet cut two keys from Books and Bites master one, but William only collected one plus the original.'

'Who told you that?'

'The young lady on the nearby fabric counter who served William when he picked up the keys.'

'Where was Jimmy?'

'On a tea break.'

'But how does the fabric woman know Jimmy cut two keys from the original?'

'She watches him like a hawk.'

'Why would she?'

Fawn laughed.

'What's so funny?'

'Have you seen Jimmy Ratchet?'

'No.'

'Take James Dean, add Brad Pitt, a tall Tom Cruise, mix in a bowl and bake on the hottest setting.'

'Quite attractive then?'

'Understatement, darling.'

It was all coming together.

'Another tomato juice, William?' I said when he returned from the loo.

'Yes – with a splash of vodka, please. Did you just mention Jimmy Ratchet?'

'Yes.'

He clutched his heart. 'Swoon – he's a dish.'

Even with the magic shortbread, I didn't dare ask my guest about vampires. But I had an idea. 'Fancy a movie, William?'

'Oh, I'd love one – I adore *Risky Business* with Tom Cruise – have you got that?'

'No. What about *Love at First Bite*?' I'd rented it on the way home.

He wrapped his arms around his tummy. 'Oh no. I've had enough of vampires.'

'Have you seen many vampire movies?'

'Er, yes, er no, not really. But some vampire movies give people the wrong idea about us, I mean, them.'

'Do you know many vampires?'

Saphira gave me a warning glare, unseen by William as if to say, *you're skating on thin fangs, Milly.*

But William said, 'Vampire movies give vampires a bad rap; I'm sure they aren't all evil.'

I gestured to the TV cabinet. 'There are a few videos in there, William – take your pick.'

He wiggled to the cabinet, opened a drawer and screamed.

Was there a rat, mouse, snake or spider in there?

'Are you okay, William?'

'Yes, yes,' he shouted as he waved a video case in the air. 'You've got *The Wizard of Oz*. Oh, I adore it and want to be Dorothy.'

He handed me the video. 'Oh, please, can we watch this, please? Tallon won't let me watch it at home – he hates Judy Garland.'

How could anyone hate Judy Garland? And I hadn't realised William lived with his creepy but handsome-hunk uncle.

William took off on a living-room circuit around the sofas as he sang, 'Follow the yellow brick road, follow the yellow brick road.' To my amusement, Saphira followed on her hind legs (unseen by William), carrying a basket, clad in a gingham dress, glittering ruby slippers on her hind paws.

I laughed so hard that William thought it was about him, picked up a banana as a microphone and launched into 'Somewhere Over the Rainbow'.

When he glanced at Saphira, her ruby slippers, dress and basket had gone, and she was just a bemused cat with a disapproving expression – a typical feline.

I'd hoped to get William's reaction to a vampire movie. Still, after this display of Judy Garland enthusiasm, I couldn't deny him *The Wizard of Oz*. So I popped the video in the slot, pressed *play*, went to the kitchen for popcorn and pop, and settled down to enjoy the movie with Saphira on my lap as I stroked her silky fur.

Whenever Toto appeared, Saphira hissed and bared her claws. Why was she so anti-dog?

I'd ask her later.

When the movie ended, William gave a huge satisfied sigh and wiped away a tear. 'Oh, that was amazing. You've got *Pretty in Pink*, too. Can I watch it another time?'

'Of course – watch it now if you like.'

I love *Pretty in Pink* and all John Hughes movies.

He pouted. 'I wish I could, but Tallon likes me in my coff ... I mean, bed before 11 pm.'

'Shall I call you a cab?'

'You're a cab,' muttered Saphira.

'Did the cat just talk?' said William.

'No – it must be your imagination. Shall I call you a cab?'

'Yes, but use Castle Cabs and put it on Tallon's account.'

'How long have you lived with your uncle?'

'Not my uncle – my boyfriend.'

Yikes.

He clapped a hand to his mouth. 'Whoops! I shouldn't have said that; Tallon pretends I'm his nephew, so please don't tell anyone.'

Tricky for me as if people tell me secrets, they are sacrosanct, and Prill said it's a rare superpower. *But should I keep this tasty morsel of paramount importance under wraps?*

As I contemplated the dilemma, Saphira winked, and I guessed it was code for, 'No – it could help crack the case.'

'What the address?'

'Radula House on Corpse Street, Patcham.'

'Corpse Street?'

'You must have misheard – *Copse* Street.'

Thank God for that – my imagination was obviously working overtime.

When William left, I said, 'Well, Saphira – his boyfriend, not uncle. And what's this about you and dogs?'

She crouched and lowered her head as if embarrassed. 'I want one.'

'Come again.'

'I want a dog.'

'But cats don't like them, particularly you.'

Sat tall and proud again, she said, 'It's not true – it's only un-evolved cats who dislike dogs, and I'm highly spiritually evolved.'

'You were pretending you don't like them as a cover-up?'

'Yes.'

'Okay, Saphira, once we sort this lot out, I'll go to Adopt-a-Dog in Brighton and get one.'

'No – do it tomorrow.'

'Why tomorrow?'

'It might help solve the current problems.'

'How?'

'Just a hunch – trust me.'

Not one to mistrust a Saphira hunch, I said, 'Yes. I'll go with Fawn tomorrow.'

'If you need me at Adopt-a-Dog, say, "Prithee Saphira, come to me," and I will appear.'

'The dogs will go crazy.'

'No, they won't as I'll be invisible and fragrance-free to most of the canines, but the correct dog will see me, hear me and like me.'

'What if I want a different dog?'

'Then get a different one, but you'll be powerless to resist my choice.'

Fascinated, I wanted to dash to Adopt-a-Dog first thing, but I'd promised to visit Fawn early.

In bed, excited and worried about the next day, I doubted I'd sleep but fell into a dreamless coma and didn't realise Robbie hadn't come home until the bedside phone rang at 7 am. Groggily, I answered, and a faint voice, Robbie's, said, 'I'm sorry, Milly. I drank too much and spent the night at Terry's.'

Although I enjoy relationship space, I dreaded this being be a regular occurrence. Was there another woman involved? My heart somersaulted at the awful thought. Another complication I didn't need. But if Robbie wanted someone else, so be it – you can't change someone's heart. But such flippancy was easier said than done.

Before he ended the call, Robbie whispered, 'I got a good price for the Aston Martin – thirty grand.'

'Wow! That's more than you said.'

'It includes commission.'

'Commission?'

'Terry has already sold it to someone else.'

'Who?'

'Tallon.'

I laughed.

'What's so funny?'

'Nothing.' I didn't mention how hilarious I found the idea of a vampire driving a white Aston Martin. Or perhaps all vampires drove Aston Martins – very paranormal James Bond.

After we said goodbye, I quickly showered, dressed in high-waist blue jeans and pink cotton jumper, hopped into my Jeep and zoomed to Fawn and Tarquin's mansion in Henfield. She'd be awake because of the jetlag.

I was right; Fawn was waiting on the lion-flanked doorstep, wrapped in a gorgeous green cashmere dressing gown. 'Come in, Milly. I've got the coffee on and croissants warming in the oven.'

The Rascals

30th October 1987

Cosy near the red Aga in Fawn's bright and cheerful kitchen, I said, 'Where's Tarquin?'

'Already at work, despite the jetlag, as he has loads of ideas for the department store. If we weren't about to run the cafe, I'd take over the boutique as it needs an introduction to 1987.'

Heck – I'd bought most of my recent clothes there; no wonder they didn't hit the mark. 'Gosh, that sounds fun.'

In the past, I'd worked in Prill's fabulous Liverpool boutique, Togs, and now sometimes missed fashion retail. However, I wasn't as clothes conscious as I'd once been.

If I worked in a boutique, perhaps the fashion enthusiasm would return. In Scone but Not Forgotten, I'd mainly worn comfy men's pleat-front trousers with a shirt or blouse tucked in. And I'd been (and now was again) so deep in murder and mayhem, I had little time or incentive to shop with the image-obsessed determination I once had, and my latest clothes were colourful but rather mumsy.

I vowed to treat myself to a London fashion spree once out of the latest pit of problems, and Tuppence was safe. But with a sharp flash of insight from deep in my subconscious, I suddenly realised that my years of lacklustre clothes choices dated back to the day I gave Tuppence away. Guilt does strange things to our psyches.

So, my embracing of funky and quirky fashions again depended on Tuppence's safety, but I would wear shapeless sackcloth dresses to ensure the latter.

'Earth to Milly,' said Fawn.

'Sorry – miles away. This coffee is delicious, as good as those you made in Scone but Not Forgotten.'

Fawn waved at a large shiny silver Gaggia coffee maker, which proudly stood on a pine worktop. 'A gift from Tarquin, and I love it.'

I was usually happy with Maxwell House instant coffee or PG Tips tea bags at home, keeping ground coffee for treats when out and about.

Plus, I didn't have Fawn's barista skills.

Recently Prill had said, 'Darling, a handsome barista made me the most sublime cappuccino in Rome yesterday.'

Confused, I answered, 'Wasn't he over-qualified?'

'What do you mean, Milly?'

'Well, you know, a barrister.'

'No, darling, b-a-r-i-s-t-a – a coffee-making expert.'

Fawn pulled me from my reverie. 'You go first, Milly.'

'First with what?'

'Don't be obtuse – what did you discover from William last night? You're usually eager to tell all but seem miles away.'

I told Fawn about Robbie going out for two nights running and not coming home on the second night.

'Isn't that what you wanted so you could sleuth without him?'

'Yes, but I can't help but worry.'

'It'll be fine – Robbie adores you. Did you glean anything from William?'

I told her about William being Tallon's boyfriend, his *Wizard of Oz* obsession, and when I mentioned Saphira and the ruby slippers, she hooted with laughter and said, 'Oh, I want a re-enactment. By the way,

Thailand was amazing – you must go, and the people are so friendly.'

'To be honest, after we solve the current problems, I'll visit mum in Florida. It's daft – I haven't gone since my windfall, and before that, it was a financial struggle.'

I imagined flying First Class as I sipped champagne and ate caviar and rather fancied the idea. Plus, I wanted to tell Mum about Tuppence in person – omitting minor (cough) details about witches and vampires. Mum would be ecstatic as she'd wanted me to keep the baby. I just hoped I could resolve Tuppence's problems soon – or at all.

'Can I come with you to Florida and we'll visit Disney World?' Fawn's eyes shone with childlike anticipation.

'Just you or you and Tarquin?'

'I wouldn't mind a girls' trip. Tarquin and I chatted on holiday and said we didn't want to become a joined-at-the-hip couple except under certain circumstances if you know what I mean.'

I certainly did, and we giggled like schoolgirls.

'I can't believe you got that information so easily,' I said.

'What information?'

'About Jimmy Ratchet.'

'Oh, that, yes. The girl from the fabric department was most helpful.'

Something dawned on me. 'Does Jimmy have black hair?'

'Yes – like a raven's wing.'

Hmm, I was sure Saphira's horror couple had a black-haired son called Jimmy. Saphira had called them the Rascals, but maybe it was a joke name for Ratchets.

'Let's visit Rich and Pour and discuss our new business over a Cheesy Chip Mountain,' said Fawn.

I stuck out my bottom lip. 'But I've just arrived and haven't had a croissant or the grand tour. Why not discuss it here?'

'Jet lag gives me ants in the pants.'

'Or all that coffee does. How many have you had this morning?

'This is my fourth, and I'm half knackered, half turbo-charged. Come on, let's get out of here.'

'Okay, we'll go and see a man or woman about a dog.'

'Come again?'

I told her of Saphira's strange request for a pet.

'That cat's a nutter.'

'Don't let her hear you say that.'

'As if I'd dare. Anyway, I'll grab a jacket, and then we'll hound hunt.'

'Let's take your Mercedes,' I teased.

'I don't want a smelly dog in my new car – your Jeep is perfect for pooches.'

On the way to the dogs' home, Fawn said, 'Have you any particular dog in mind – tiny, small, giant, medium-size, chihuahua, Saint Bernard?

'Saphira said I'll know it when I see it.'

'I knew the right man when I saw him.'

'So Tarquin is the one?'

'Yes.'

'That's nice.'

'He proposed in Thailand, and I said yes.'

So pleased I nearly swerved into a tree, I shouted, 'Wow – congratulations – I'm over the moon.'

I genuinely was – they were lovely together.

'Thanks.'

But her voice had a melancholy tone.

'What's up, Fawn?'

She hesitated. 'It's daft.'

'Try me.'

'I wish Tarquin wasn't so rich.'

'Why?'

'I just wish we were on more equal footing because all that money makes me feel a little inferior, at a disadvantage, and I don't need all that showy wealth.'

'So you'll just have a tiny diamond chip in your faux-gold engagement ring,' I teased.

'Don't be daft – I've already chosen a whopping enormous diamond, surrounded by rubies.'

Not so worried about Tarquin's wealth, then? I suppressed a smile. 'Where from?'

'His mum's safe. It was that or a massive sapphire surrounded by diamonds.'

'Why aren't you wearing it?'

'It needs sizing.'

'Come on, Fawn, let's go adopt a dog.'

'Okay – but I'll stay in the car as it must be your choice. Besides, I want to read *Hollywood Husbands* – I'm on a juicy bit.'

I guessed the real reason was she'd want all the dogs, and her tender heart wouldn't cope.

Prospero

After I gave my details to the friendly woman at the Adopt-a-Dog front desk, she walked me around the kennels. All the residents were cute, and it was impossible to decide.

Then I saw him – the friendliest, cutest dog I'd ever encountered. His black and white face lit up in a loopy grin, and he showed no trepidation or fear and ran towards me, stood on his long hind legs and licked my hand ecstatically through the metal mesh. It was like we'd known each other for years.

If this weren't the right dog, I'd gladly donate my entire fortune to these premises. Whatever, I'd make a generous donation – or 'dognation'.

'Oh, he's gorgeous,' I said.

'How do you know it's a he?'

'He's got a beard.'

Realising the joke, the assistant slapped an ample thigh as I said, 'It's obvious he's male.'

'How?'

Had nobody taught this woman the facts of life?

I nodded towards the dog's evident excitement.

'Oh, I see.' She turned bright red.

'I'll call him Prospero. Can I take him today?' I said.

Prospero? Where did that come from? Probably from all the force-feeding of Shakespeare in school. A snippet from *The Tempest* popped into my head...

> *To work mine end upon their senses that*
> *This airy charm is for, I'll break my staff,*
> *Bury it certain fathoms in the earth,*
> *And deeper than did ever plummet sound*
> *I'll drown my book.*

But I must have muttered the verse out loud as the assistant said, 'What book will you drown?'

My face burned. 'Oh, sorry, just recalling Prospero's namesake. May I take him today?'

'No – you must fill in the forms and come back tomorrow.'

Prospero had to be freed that day – or Saphira would drive me nuts.

Under my breath, I muttered, 'Prithee Saphira, come to me,' and in moments, she was a cat amongst the pigeons – or a cat amongst the dogs. In normal circumstances, this would drive the tenants wild, but as I've said, Saphira was no ordinary cat. And I thought Prospero was a regular dog, albeit extra friendly, until he said to Saphira, 'What took you so long?'

'Hello to you, too,' said Saphira snootily.

Thankfully the assistant seemed oblivious. 'Fill in the forms, and after a few checks, you may pick up Prospero tomorrow.'

'I want out of this cage now,' said Prospero.

'Wait a minute,' Saphira hissed. 'I'll sort it. Hangfire for another few minutes.'

In the office, as I filled out forms, Saphira said, 'Ask again if you can take Prospero today, Milly.'

I didn't want to, as the formerly friendly assistant appeared scarily adamant. And although my confidence had increased due to the magic shortbread and various circumstances, I could still be wimpish.

'No,' I mouthed

'Go on,' urged Saphira.

Like Oliver Twist requesting more gruel, I nervously begged, 'Please, may I take him today?'

Saphira waved a paw as luminous pink stars fizzled from it, floated across the room, rose, and sank into the assistant's head.

Face wrinkled with confusion, she said, 'Oh, I don't see why not. The dog obviously adores you already – I've seen nothing like it before.'

Result.

Within ten minutes, Fawn, Prospero, and I were zooming to Piddleton-on-Sea in the Jeep. Saphira had disappeared again.

We'd got ourselves a dog.

Then I remembered I hadn't asked Robbie – how rude and presumptuous.

Tense from worry and guilt, I gripped the steering wheel tight.

'What's up?' said Fawn. 'Your knuckles have turned white. Prospero isn't a scary Rottweiler, more like a sheepdog cross.'

'Bearded collie, Lurcher cross, your friendly neighbourhood pooch,' added Prospero.

'Did you hear that?' I asked Fawn.

She looked up from *Hollywood Husbands*. 'Hear what?'

'Nothing.' Perhaps I was going mad.

A talking cat was crazy enough and now a talking dog. What next? A talking horse? The fantastic *Mister Ed* was one of my favourite shows as a kid. *Don't yell at me, Wilbur – I'm not your wife.*

Fawn chirped up, 'Spill, Milly. What's the problem, and why are you so nervous?'

Whether she'd heard Prospero talk or not – how was Fawn so nonchalant about him? She'd often told me about her beloved childhood dog, and how sad she was when he died.

Perhaps that was it – maybe she'd never got over it.

Realising I hadn't answered Fawn, I said, 'I didn't tell Robbie I was getting a dog.'

'You're not – I am,' piped up Saphira, who had appeared again. 'But no worries, I heard Robbie on the phone to Terry yesterday saying he'd love a dog but didn't think you did.'

Problem solved. But maybe Robbie wouldn't have chosen Prospero; then again, how could he resist?

A cunning idea formed. 'Fawn, how about a little subterfuge?'

I told her my plan, and she said, 'Naughty, but nice – I love it.'

Then she winked at Prospero.

'Why did you wink at the dog?' I said.

'Don't be silly – I had something in my eye.'

Gosh – I was becoming paranoid

Instead of going straight to Piddleton-on-Sea, we parked near Brighton Lanes, lucky to get a spot without going into the underground car park, and walked towards Rich and Pour, careful to saunter by Robbie's shop, hoping he saw us. He did and rushed out saying, 'Whose is the gorgeous dog?'

As Prospero stuck his nose in the air, obviously pleased at the compliment, Fawn sneezed loudly then said, 'Mine, but unfortunately, I must find a new owner.'

When two fat tears plopped onto her cheeks, followed by several smaller ones, I was impressed by her thespian ability. '...And the best actress award goes to...'

'Why must you find a new owner, Fawn?' Robbie's eyes filled with canine-wanting hope.

'An allergy – sometimes happens with long-haired dogs.'

Robbie gave me a questioning look, and I nodded. 'Yes, okay, Robbie. Prospero is rather hard to resist.'

He punched the air. 'Yes! Where are you off to, Milly?'

'Rich and Pour – they allow dogs.'

As I tried not to laugh at Prospero's outraged expression at 'allow dogs', Robbie pulled a key from a trouser pocket and said, 'I'll lock up and come with you.'

However, a glamorous young woman appeared. 'Oh, are you closing? I've come for the doggie in the window.'

Sure enough, at centre space was a ceramic bearded collie.

I giggled. 'If you don't make the cafe before we leave, Robbie, we'll swing by and say hi.'

In Rich and Pour, Prospero was a hit, and everyone wanted to pat him.

But Hamish seemed sheepish. 'Can I have a word with you, Milly and Fawn? Outside if it's okay?'

Oh, no, what now?

Change of Plan

We left Prospero with his admirers, and outside Rich and Pour, Hamish twisted his apron nervously. 'I've changed my mind about the cafe. Have you signed the lease?'

'No, we're about to sign it later,' said Fawn. 'Why have you changed your mind?'

'When push comes to shove, I can't bear to leave.' Hamish swallowed a sob, pulled a large blue hanky from his jeans pocket, and gave a hefty blow.

I looked at Fawn, and she nodded, winked, then said. 'Can Milly and I have a few moments alone?'

'Sure.'

'I've had an idea,' Fawn said when Hamish left.

'Go on...'

'Do you want to run the cafe, Milly, or do you have doubts?'

'Yes.'

'Yes, you want the cafe, or yes, you have doubts?'

'The last one.'

'Then here's my plan...'

I liked it.

Fawn went indoors and sent Hamish outside to me.

Fingers crossed mentally, I said, 'Hamish, we're disappointed but partly relieved as we've had an idea for a new business.'

'What is it?'

'I don't suppose you know of the shortbread biscuits everyone was crazy about when Fawn and I ran Scone but Not Forgotten in London?'

'Not until this morning when a cheeky customer commented that mine are awful in comparison.'

'Fawn and I want to make them commercially. If we forgo the lease, will you buy a batch from us every morning?'

Without waiting to think, he said, 'It would be my pleasure.'

Back in Rich and Pour, I snuggled into a seat and sipped the cappuccino Fawn had ordered.

'It's not as good as mine,' she said modestly.

'But still nice,' I defended Rita. Was Rita disappointed that Hamish cancelled the move to Scotland? Better not ask, as it might be a touchy subject.

Then Saphira appeared and whispered in my ear, 'Hurry home, Milly, as I want to chat with Prospero privately. And don't look so worried – apart from you and Fawn, humans can't see or hear me at the moment. She winked, blew a kiss then vanished.

'Oh, look, here's Tuppence,' said Fawn as my heart leapt with hope. Was she off the hook?

A smiling Tuppence sat beside me and bent to stroke Prospero. 'What a gorgeous dog. What's her name?

I laughed. 'Prospero. How could you mistake this handsome boy for a girl?'

'I'm still woozy from being in a cell.'

'Have they found the real culprit?' I said, fingers crossed under the table.

My daughter's gorgeous face clouded. 'No, but my darling aunt got me out on massive bail. Mum wanted to but hasn't the funds since Dad lost all their money nine years ago on a bad investment. He committed suicide, and Mum downsized from a huge house to a tiny one.'

I was sad about Tuppence's dad, but for the moment, I didn't give a damn where Tuppence's mum lived. Tuppence's mum – I was her natural mother but lost the right to be *Mum* when I gave her away, and my heart clenched with sorrow and regret.

'Why do they think you murdered Simon?' I said softly.

'The pathologist said it wasn't a heart attack and found traces of succitupamine in Simon's last coffee, enough to kill two men. Worse, they found a vial of the stuff in my handbag.'

My pulse raced with worry for my daughter. 'Think back, Tuppence. Did anyone else touch that coffee before you handed it to Simon?'

'Only Rita, but she made it.'

We all looked at Rita. Was she an evil poisoner? Was that why Hamish had cancelled Scotland? Had he discovered his beloved was a murderer? Rita saw us watching her, stomped over and said, 'What's up?'

As it was a matter of life and death – Tuppence's, I said, 'What do you remember about the morning Simon died? Someone poisoned his coffee.'

'Are you accusing me?' she said, expression murderous, hands on her ample hips.

'No, but Tuppence's freedom is at stake,' Fawn said.

Rita sat on a nearby vacant chair, held her chin and looked upwards. 'Hang on a mo – I remember now.' She looked at Tuppence. 'It was mad busy, and I told that handsome lad, Jimmy, who works on Henderson's key-cutting counter, to deliver it to your table on the way out. He'd popped in for his usual bacon sandwich.'

We had probably solved the case.

But how to prove it?

As I mulled, Rita said, 'Jimmy's a nice boy. Unusual, as he's part of that awful Ratchet family, and they're a nasty bunch. If he did anything bad, I bet he was bribed or blackmailed.'

How astute Rita was and how silly I hadn't quizzed her earlier. But I wasn't a clever detective, just someone who kept landing in murderous mires. I hoped this was the last one, as I'd had more than enough.

'Some evil property man called Reggie Ratchet was once murdered with poisoned coffee.' I said.

'Ooh, I remember that from the newspapers,' said Rita. 'Must go – there's a queue at the counter.'

When she left, Fawn said, 'We should go to the police, tell them right away.'

Tuppence put a hand on my arm. 'It's time I came clean.'

Did she know I was her mum? 'What about?'

'I saw and heard a beautiful Siamese cat say goodbye to you then disappear, so I guess one of you is a witch?'

'Why would you say that?' I said.

'Because I'm a witch.'

I couldn't say I already knew. Besides, I wanted evidence. 'Prove it.'

Tuppence wrinkled her pretty brow. 'My magic powers have faded lately, but hang on a minute and let me focus.'

We waited until Tuppence nodded her head towards Union Street and said, 'See that middle-aged woman in the navy and white suit looking in the Baubles and Beads window?'

'Yes,' said Fawn and I.

'Keep looking – the suit will turn red and white for a few seconds.'

To my amazement, it did.

'Convinced?' said Tuppence.

We nodded.

'Which one of you is a witch?' added Tuppence.

'Neither of us,' replied Fawn. 'But Mum is head of the WFGC.'

'Heck – The Witches For Good Council – poor you – I heard she's a stickler for rules.'

Fawn groaned. 'Tell me about it.'

'And you, Milly?' said Tuppence. 'What's your magic connection?'

I briefly explained Prill, Bill, Saphira and my recent past.

'Now it's my turn to explain,' said Tuppence. 'And also tell you my suspicions.'

Prospero gave me a pleading glance, and I bent towards him. 'I need a tree or a lamppost fast,' he whispered.

'Fancy coming back to my place, Fawn and Tuppence?' I said. 'We'll make plans there, and I'll drop you both home later.'

We grabbed our bags and jackets then said goodbye to Rita and Hamish. 'I'll deliver the first batch of shortbread tomorrow,' I told them.

Rita gave Hamish a questioning glance.

'I'll explain later, sweetheart,' he said fondly.

Ah, they were still in love, and my heart turned over.

Chez Milly

Oh, I love this house, Milly – it's so airy, bright and cheerful,' said Tuppence. 'Simon's place, The Friary, was so gloomy and spooky in comparison.'

'Have you moved out?' I said.

'My stuff is still there, but I'm back in Mum's little semi-detached house in Hove, and my David Bowie and Led Zeppelin posters are still on my bedroom wall. Before Simon changed personality, we had plans to lighten the Friary's decor, but afterwards, he wanted it gloomier with dimmer lighting.'

Gosh – I hadn't envisaged teenage Tuppence as a Bowie and Led Zep fan, more Bay City Rollers, and it showed we can't always judge people by their musical tastes. 'Did Simon's personality change dramatically?' I said.

She picked at her floral needlecord skirt. 'It's more than that – and I haven't admitted it to myself before, but I'm not sure he was even the same person.'

This equated with what I'd thought when she showed me the photograph.

'The thing is,' she continued as her voice cracked, 'I reckon the real Simon and the fake Simon are both dead.'

I went along with her theory. 'Do you know of anyone who looked similar to the real Simon?'

'He once mentioned an older cousin who resembled him when they were kids. However, Simon hadn't heard from him since he moved to Eastern Europe years ago.'

Eastern Europe? Transylvania? Yikes.

'Any idea what happened to him?' I said.

'No – but I'll ask Simon's mum, discover what she knows. It's a double-edged sword as I don't want to give her false hope, seeing as it's a long shot and possibly just my wishful imagination.'

'Did you love Simon before he changed, or an imposter stepped in?' I doubted her theory but wanted to be open-minded.

'Adored him, and that's why I lied to myself, told myself it was a blip, and he'd return to being my darling boy. But let's face it, he wasn't Simon, but a vampire. Look!' She pulled down her pink polo-neck collar to show two vivid red puncture marks.

Almost lost for words, I said, 'Perhaps the real Simon is still alive?'

'Oh, please God.'

'Tell us about him,' Fawn interjected.

Tuppence hesitated. 'I'm uncertain of my theory – perhaps I'm grasping at slender straws that my Simon is alive. Anyway, he was a serious soul but genuine, not a dishonest bone in his body, and so kind.'

'Kindness is paramount,' I said.

'I know, but the changed or replaced version was horrid.'

Saphira yawned then said, 'Paramount is to prove Tuppence didn't kill Simon, whatever version he was.'

Fawn bit her lip. 'I'm confused.'

'You and me both, but let's try to summarise,' I replied.

Saphira tutted. 'No – I will – you silly humans embellish every-thing and make a drama about a trip to the corner shop.'

I folded my arms. 'Go on then, Miss Saphira Succinct. Perhaps you should start an incident board.'

'Pah – with my brilliant brain, silly props are worthless. Do I have the stage?'

'Always.'

I rolled my eyes as Fawn whispered, 'Talk about the kettle call-ing the pot black – Saphira is such a drama queen.'

'It's the other way round,' I added, 'The pot calls the kettle black.'

'What a pointless exchange of triviality,' said Saphira. 'Now, here is the situation as I infer it – vampires are the root of the prob-lem and probably had a hand, or a fang, in Simon's murder. They want to take over Brighton by any means.'

'And William is Tallon's boyfriend and, for whatever reason, half bitten or newish, is still rather sweet,' said Fawn.

Saphira nodded. 'I agree. He's too nice to be in full vampire mode and still eats human food.'

'So he could be a half-vampire?' I said.

'Quick, aren't you?' said Saphira.

'Can it, cat!'

She tried to hide a smirk but failed. Saphira loved backtalk, or my life might have been a misery.

'Sorry to be selfish,' began Tuppence, 'but surely the priority is to get me off the hook. Plus, oh, this is awful, but I'm craving blood, so where does that leave me? Even if I don't go to prison, I can't face being a vampire and would rather die. In Brighton Lanes, a little boy fell and cut his knee a few days ago, and I wanted to lick the wound despite finding the idea macabre and repulsive.'

This was too awful – I could not let my darling daughter become a vampire, and my tummy clenched with terror.

Fawn frowned. 'Mum never tells me much about witchy stuff, but after a large sherry, she let something slip about vampire reversal.'

'And Prill also said vampire reversal is possible,' I added, not wishing to overstate the case lest the spell was ineffective or, worse, impossible due to location, circumstance and timing.

'Changing the subject slightly,' said Fawn. 'Surely they would know if Simon *is* Simon from dental records and stuff.'

'Who are *they*?' I said.

'The police, silly.'

'Not necessarily,' said Tuppence. 'Simon's mum, Effie, is into alternative therapy, so he never visited conventional doctors. When he had colitis at ten years old, she took him to India to see some renowned Ayurvedic doctor who cured him with herbs and diet. Also, Simon has dentophobia and has never visited a dentist.'

I imagined two rows of rotting teeth. 'What did Simon do for a toothache?' I said but regretted the past tense when I noticed Tuppence's stricken expression.

She recovered then said, 'The lucky duck has never had a toothache. Before he turned nasty, we threw a dinner party, and one guest was a dentist. She couldn't believe he'd never sat in a dentist's chair – in a professional capacity, of course. So, when we'd all drunk too much champagne, she made him open his mouth as I shone a pink Maglite torch into it. And she couldn't believe it.'

'That it was so awful?' I asked.

'No – that his teeth were perfect with nary a cavity. And, I just remembered – the dinner-party dentist said something odd.'

What?' I said.

Tuppence hugged herself. 'She said, "You'd make a perfect vampire, Simon, with those lovely sharp eye teeth. Most people would get them capped these days, but I find them attractive." Then she nuzzled near his neck and whispered something in his ear. The familiarity miffed me.'

Tuppence clapped a hand to her mouth. 'Oh, no, perhaps she bit Simon surreptitiously and turned him into a vampire.'

'Surely you'd have noticed bite marks?' I said.

'I suppose, although Simon usually wore silk cravats.'

True. Simon sported a red and blue silk one when I first saw him.

'Surely he didn't wear them in bed?' I ventured – the idea was crazy.

After some hesitation, Tuppence snapped, 'Yes, he did – with his pyjamas.'

Most odd, and the hairs at the back of my neck prickled as I wondered if Tuppence *was* Simon's murderer – and couldn't keep track of the lies. Who would wear a cravat to bed?

Then the answer came to me – Bertie Wooster – so perhaps Simon was simply quaint, upper class and old-fashioned.

Fawn grinned widely. 'I just had a strong intuition about Simon.'

'Spill,' said Saphira.

'His mum knows something.'

Tuppence's eyes brightened. 'I bet you're right as Effie adored her son – the nice version of Simon – and they had a wonderful connection. But she barely looked at the horrid version. And if the genuine Simon were murdered, she'd hunt me down to find the truth, but I haven't heard a dicky bird. Oh, Simon might be alive – deep joy. Oh, but it's no use.'

My heart ached to witness my daughter's grief, and I threw my doubts about her innocence to the winds. 'What's no use?'

She smiled to show two little fangs. 'I'm more of a vampire every day, and perhaps I'm grasping at flimsy straws about Simon being alive.'

It was too much for me, and I muttered, 'Prithee, Prill, come to me.'

In a mystical puff of pink and blue smoke, Prill appeared and said, 'We need some perspective here. It's easy to lose it as it's nearly Halloween, which reduces brain coherence for mere mortals, never mind witches and extra-special cat familiars. But we have too many cooks spoiling the cauldron broth, so I'll give a little perspective.'

'What makes you immune to the pre-Halloween craziness?' said Saphira, back arched.

'Being dead, dear.'

That stopped the sassy cat in her tracks, and Prill continued, 'So, I shall lead this investigation.'

First, she addressed Tuppence. 'Visit Simon's mum, discover what she knows and if she's hiding anything. Milly will gift wrap a few shortbread biscuits for you – pink cellophane with a big purple organza bow works well.'

'I don't have cellophane and organza,' I said.

Prill waved a hand as rolls of pink cellophane, and purple ribbon appeared on the coffee table. 'You do now, Milly, and with Saphira's help, bake a batch of magic shortbread for Rich and Pour and use double the usual magic essence. Vampire and other dark energies are extra powerful right now, and mortals' positivity from shortbread consumption will help thwart danger and evil forces. Would you please deliver the shortbread to Rich and Pour first thing tomorrow morning?'

I saluted. 'Aye aye, sir.'

Fawn raised her eyebrows. 'What about me, Prill?'

'Discover what you can from Tarquin – his family has lived in Brighton for years. Enquire about the Ratchets. And, tomorrow morning, when Jimmy visits Rich and Pour for his usual bacon sandwich, flutter your eyelashes and ask him to join you.'

'How do you know his routine?'

'I haven't been idle, darling.'

Fawn blushed prettily. 'No, of course not, but why would he sit with me?'

'Have you looked in the mirror lately, darling?' Prill shook her head and said, 'Deary me, youth truly is wasted on the young.'

'What if Jimmy's worried about getting back to work?' added Fawn.

'Say his job's safe, and if he helps you, you'll recommend him for promotion.'

'To what?' said Fawn. 'Master key cutter?'

Prill grinned. 'I'm sure you can persuade Tarquin to promote him or give him a small raise. That's if Jimmy Ratchet isn't the culprit, and they promote him to prison.'

Stupidly, I hadn't considered this scenario. Of course, even if someone had coerced Jimmy to spike the drink and plant evidence on Tuppence, he was still guilty of conspiracy to murder or whatever the official term was.

'What else should I do?' I asked Prill.

'Go to Instaprinters after you deliver the shortbread and order one hundred invitations to a Halloween party in Fawn's house tomorrow night.'

In my confusion, I'd forgotten it was Halloween the next day. 'Why are we throwing a party?' I said.

'You'll see.' Prill touched the side of her nose.

'Isn't it late notice?'

'Most invitees will accept – even Tallon and William, and if our enquiries go as I imagine, I'll set a trap.'

'What sort of trap?'

Prill looked at the sleeping dog fondly and said, 'You'll see.'

'What if Tarquin refuses to throw a party in our home?' said Fawn.

'Do you think he will?'

'No way. I've got the poor man around my little finger.'

Prill grinned. 'There you go.'

'What about catering?' I asked.

'It's strange, but Tarquin and I planned an engagement party for tomorrow night, but our friends broke up yesterday after Tarquin paid the caterers. I'll add a Halloween twist and have spooky fun with the decor. I noticed some huge rolls of black net and red tulle in Henderson's fabric department and some wonderful spiders, webs, skeletons, witch hats, and stuff in the toy department,' said Fawn.

Seeing Prill's wily grin, I wondered what part she'd played in the engagement party cancellation. 'Good,' she said. 'Let's arrive at Tarquin and Fawn's house an hour before the party for a run-through. Oh, also Fawn, to make sure Tallon accepts, offer him fifty per cent off new carpeting for Books and Bites.'

'So, I should invite him, not Milly?' said Fawn.

Prill hesitated. 'No, Milly should invite him and pass on the message.'

Drat – I thought I was off the vampire hook.

'You need organising, Prill,' said Saphira. 'Your mind is incoherent because of pre-Halloween craziness.'

I laughed, then said, 'I presume we should dress up, Prill?'

'Of course, it's a party – oh, I almost forgot – bring Prospero.'

I wanted to anyway, but why make a point of it? 'Why bring him, Prill?'

'He likes parties.'

Saphira swished her tail angrily. 'What about me?'

'Do what you want – you always do, darling,' Prill said fondly.

'Will there be a denouement?' I said.

Prill raised a brow. 'A denouement, darling?'

'Yes, like at the end of Agatha Christie novels.'

'I know what one is – but wait and see.'

'Shall I bring Robbie?'

'Of course – he's your husband, not a toddler.'

'No, I mean should I bring him to the pre-party meeting?'

'Yes.'

'But he doesn't know about all the magic and that you're a ghost and...'

'Just bring him, darling, and all will fall into place.'

Prill issued more instructions, then winked and disappeared in a purple star-filled cloud, leaving many questions in my mind.

After I dropped everyone off then drove home, Saphira and I began our next task, but the usually cheeky cat was subdued, and I missed her overdrive of sass. Usually, as I mixed the shortbread and added the magical essence, Saphira recited silly verses and channelled Veronica Lake on the kitchen counter. Now all she did was mutter under her breath and wave a languid paw.

I stated the obvious. 'You're not yourself.'

'I know. We need to de-vampire Tallon for good. His power has grown since the last time I met him, and even then, it was hideous.'

My heart nearly stopped. 'Will we win?'

'Good always wins over evil, eventually.'

My scalp prickled – *eventually* wasn't good enough. 'But we must win tomorrow.'

'Let's hope, Milly, let's hope, or my talking-cat days are over, and I'll turn to dust.'

I dropped the wooden spoon. 'No, Saphira, I couldn't bear it.'

'What couldn't you bear, Milly?' Robbie walked into the kitchen to see me baking and a normal if dejected cat on the kitchen counter.

I thought fast. 'If this batch of biscuits failed.'

He frowned. 'It's unlike you to act all Mrs Beeton, Milly – it's only a few biscuits.'

'No – it's my new enterprise. Fawn and I will supply them to Rich and Pour, then maybe Books and Bites.' If William could persuade Tallon, he'd bite my hand off to stock the shortbread biscuits, and it would be a great way to dispel dark vampire energies.

'But I thought you and Fawn were taking over Rich and Pour.'

'Long story and I'll tell you later.'

Much later.

'Okay. I'm off to play with Prospero, then take him for a walk before dinner. Where is he?'

'Fast asleep on our bed.'

Prill had said Prospero was tired after his recent experiences, but she didn't embellish, apart from saying he'd need all his energy for the party.

What was going on?

On the one hand, I wanted to know; on the other, ignorance was, as they say, bliss. Besides, I had enough on my plate.

Halloween

31st October 1987

I leapt from bed the moment the radio alarm woke me with Wet Wet Wet's 'Sweet Little Mystery'.

There was nothing sweet about the current mysteries.

Robbie groaned. 'Come back for a cuddle, Milly, as I'm not in the shop today.'

'Sorry – too much to do.' I pulled on stone-wash jeans and a yellow sweatshirt and said, 'Will you take Prospero for a quick constitutional?'

'Yes – after a long walk over Devil's Dyke, I'll take him to the Shepherd and Dog in my latest car.'

Robbie's current chariot was a cute green 1950s Riley saloon – quite a contrast from the Aston Martin. 'The pub in Fulking?'

'Yes – I had a beer last night, and Prospero seemed desperate to get at it, so I popped some in a bowl, and he lapped it up along with a few beef-flavour crisps.'

'Don't get him drunk – he has a party to attend later.'

'Party? What party?'

'You're invited too.'

'Gee, thanks – I'm honoured to be up there with the dog.'

'Cheek,' said Prospero, who had just padded in. He put a paw to his lips as if to say, *whoops*.

'Did Prospero just speak?' said Robbie.

'Don't be silly; he's a dog – that was me practising a deep voice.'

'What is the party in aid of, anyway?'

'A Halloween bash – at Tarquin's place.'

Robbie continued his mock sulk as he patted Prospero. 'Sounds good, but it's nice to be an afterthought.'

'You're never an afterthought, darling. A naughty image of you is always at the forefront of my dirty mind.'

Robbie grinned wickedly. 'Do I dress up for this party?'

'Up to you – but perhaps your black skinny-rib sweater and those thigh-hugging black jeans.'

'I'll look like that daft Milk-Tray man.'

'Not a bad thing.' I loved the silly but sexy adverts featuring a handsome James-Bond-like character dressed in black. The determined man skied deep and treacherous slopes, dived off cliffs, steered speedboats and leapt from speeding cars in his relentless quest to deliver a box of chocolates to some lucky woman.

'Add horns to make you spookier,' I said.

'I don't have horns.'

'I'll get you a pair from that place in town.'

'Fancy That on North Street?'

'That's the one.'

'Oh, and a tail.'

'You devil!'

'I'll buy a hearse to drive to the party in.'

'You're kidding.'

'Not necessarily. There's big money in hearses, and Tarquin has some for sale.'

'Why would Tarquin's own hearses? It seems dead silly to me.'

Robbie groaned. 'You don't know about his funeral business?'

'No, I didn't – he has a finger in every coffin.'

'True – anyway, he's replacing his funeral fleet.'

With a shudder, I said, 'Don't tell me more.'

'So I shouldn't buy a hearse?'

'No – too much like tempting fate – the final journey in a death limo is enough.' Chilly at the morbid thought, I shook my head to dispel the terror.

'Can Terry come to the party, Milly?'

'You sound five – Mum, can I bring my friend?'

With a wry grin, Robbie said, 'But can he, oh powerful one?'

'Already on the list – he and Audrey.'

I sped into Brighton in the Jeep, parked, ran to Rich and Pour and handed Hamish the shortbread.

Next stop – Instaprinters.

The tall, muscular young man at the counter seemed more interested in studying his luminous green nails than in serving me.

'What can I do you for?' he said lazily.

Why did people say that instead of *what can I do for you*? It irritated me, or perhaps I was stroppy because of circumstances.

'I need a hundred invitations printed for a Halloween party.'

He yawned. '31st October is today.'

What a genius. 'No kidding.'

'It's short notice, is all I'm saying.'

'Your sign says you can print two hundred invitations within an hour.'

'No, I mean short notice for the party.'

Spontaneously I said, 'You can come if you like.'

The cocky manner crumpled as his broad shoulders slumped. 'Oh, I'm not sure.'

He was probably a handsome man beneath the scowl, pale foundation and black eyeliner. 'Bring a friend – or a *fiend* as it's Halloween,' I said.

His expressive eyes filled with tears. 'I planned to stay home with popcorn and a movie, *Carry on Screaming* perhaps, because I lost my boyfriend last Halloween, and I'd cry and make a fool of myself in public.'

'Oh, I'm so sorry. How did he die?'

'He didn't, but he's dead to me – ran off with an older, richer man.'

'Oh, I'm sorry. Does he still live around here?'

'Yes, he runs Books and Bites for his boyfriend, who is rather scary and yonks older than him – looks like he's been embalmed.'

Could it be?

'Was your boyfriend called William.'

'He's still called William, although I call him The Traitor.'

'He'll be at the party. Why don't you come?'

'I'd feel like an idiot.'

'Why?'

'I'm the jilted party.'

'Have you got a new boyfriend?'

'Yes, he's gorgeous, but I don't love him like I loved William – William, and I giggled all the time, but although my new boyfriend looks amazing, he's boring and doesn't kiss like William.'

Yes – he still loved William – he'd said his beloved's name three times in one sentence. 'Bring your gorgeous new boyfriend, as it might make William jealous,' I said.

'I might come. Thanks.'

While I waited for the invites, I nipped to Rich and Pour for a mug of tea and a little snack. Fawn was there and winked at me from across the room, but I sat at a different table as she was on a mission.

I was somewhat disappointed Fawn and I wouldn't run Rich and Pour, as it had a wonderful convivial vibe. Then again, I could enjoy it as a punter with no business worries attached.

As I devoured cherry pie smothered in fresh cream – utter heaven – a handsome young man who fitted Fawn's description of Jimmy Ratchet to a tee (Take James Dean, add Brad Pitt, a tall Tom Cruise, mix in a bowl and bake on the hottest setting) strode in and hastened to the counter.

On his way out, Fawn batted her eyelashes and said something I couldn't hear. He hesitated, blushed crimson, then sat with her. Yes - it had to be Jimmy Ratchet.

Cherry pie already wolfed down, I lingered over my tea, hoping to catch up with Fawn, but when it was time to collect the invites, she and Jimmy were still chatting.

The invitations were perfect – printed on thick white cards with carbon-black raised letters, vampire bats around the edges. At the base of the invites, it said, *Attend, or an evil witch will turn you into a frog.*

I paid the young man and said, 'What's your name for the invite?'

'Phoenix.'

I hastily wrote his name and handed him an invitation. 'Hope to see you later, Phoenix,' then dashed away to begin delivery.

Perhaps he'd live up to his name, rise from the ashes and rekindle his relationship with William.

'It's a bit late notice,' some commented, or a variation of, but when most noticed the party was at Tarquin's, they said, 'Perhaps I can change plans.'

The power of money. Or perhaps it was simply that Fawn and Tarquin were popular.

It was lucky Halloween wasn't as big a thing in the UK as in the USA, and most people stayed in and watched a scary movie while they waited for trick or treaters to knock at their doors. So it was easy for most people to cancel such a plan. Most years, no trick or treaters arrived, and I ate mountains of sweets and chocolate myself during the following days – a terrible hardship.

I hesitated at the scariest place of all – Transylvanian Trinkets. I was TERRIFIED when I went in, and Tallon towered behind his vast ebony desk like Count Dracula in his castle as poor William cowered in his evil shadow.

William had said he was helping in Tallon's shop until the new carpet was fitted in Books and Bites.

When I handed them an invitation apiece, Tallon spat in strong Eastern European tones, 'Ve do not party with peasants. And who vould dare turn Tallon into a frog – if they did, I vould turn them into scorpions.' Then he cackled as William shrank away further.

Gosh – how rude and nasty Tallon was.

'If you check the address, sir, you'll see the party is at Tarquin Henderson's home. Tarquin learned of your carpet plight and now offers you a fifty per cent discount for the floor covering of your choice,' I said nervously.

'I vant blood-red Vilton decorated with cute black coffin motifs to match the cafe's theme, as I intend to focus on spooky, spine-chilling books to thrill the customers.'

Terrify them, more like.

'I can't afford Wilton, even at half price,' whispered William. 'On my wages, I'll be paying for it for years.'

'Hush, boy, and only speak vhen spoken to,' spat Tallon. 'Your vages are generous, and you get free room and board.'

'Free coffin and board, more like,' muttered William.

Goodness, it was like something from a Charles Dickens novel – *Extra-Bleak House*, perhaps.

Poor William would beg for gruel next. 'Please, sir, may I have more gruel with a drizzle of virgin's blood?'

The thought turned my tummy.

After distributing more invitations to happy recipients and a curmudgeon or three, I had fun in Fancy That, where I chose a gorgeous, luxurious to the touch, red and black velvet vampire dress and a long black wig. I also treated myself to a hauntingly musky fragrance called Eau de Graveyard, white foundation, plastic fangs, and vampire-red lipstick.

A few invitees were in the shop, and the proprietor, dressed as Frankenstein, seemed pleased. 'We haven't been this busy on Halloween for years. Is there a special event?'

I fished an invitation from my bag. 'Yes – this.'

His eyes glinted with excitement. 'Oh, I'd love to come and don't wish to be a frog.'

I laughed. 'Tell you what, offer anyone who's coming to the party a twenty per cent discount on Halloween outfits, and an invitation is yours. Bring a guest.'

'Done.' He shook my hand.

I heard a familiar voice and turned to see a grinning Terry who said, 'Ah, the Brighton Lanes barter system is rubbing off on you. Twenty per cent off, eh? Perhaps I'll choose the velour imp outfit rather than the nylon. Audrey has gone to Harrods for her outfit – she'll only wear designer clothes, but no matter, I love her. Besides, I had to make amends as she's furious with me.'

'What did you do?' I said.

'Invited a few young ladies around for naked tennis last month while Audrey was at her mother's in Chichester, and she hasn't forgiven me.'

'That was ballsy of you, Terry. Did you tell her about it, or did someone else?' I wondered if he had enemies.

'Didn't have to, darling, she arrived home unexpectedly when it was forty love. It's cost me a pretty packet since – four designer handbags, endless clothes and shoes. But I've ordered her a heart pendant with our names entwined on it in diamonds – that should do it. If it doesn't, I might need a little magic.'

He didn't need an imp outfit as he was already wicked. And I hoped he wasn't corrupting Robbie and doubted Audrey would like the pendant.

When I left Fancy That, a hunch told me to head to Sweetie Pie.

Tuppence

Butterflies fluttered in my tummy as I approached Effie's cottage. What if she blamed me for her son's death? But it was a relief to have Milly on my side – I liked her loads, and it was as if I'd known her for years.

I didn't murder Simon, really, I didn't – his character changed, and I'd wanted to escape, but a dark force stopped me. Perhaps my vampire bite, which Simon (horrid version) swore was an insect bite, caused the darkness.

'This vampire business is hysterical nonsense, Tuppence, and if you continue this female hysteria, I'll commit you to an asylum.'

As my throat contracted with terror, I'd whispered, 'This isn't Victorian times – asylums don't exist, and you don't have the power.'

'It's a secret asylum where nobody will hear your screams. But the hot and cold water therapy should cure your delusions. If not, then perhaps electric shock therapy.'

As I'd stifled a terrified whimper, he pasted a fake smile on his demonic face and said, 'You'll feel better after we marry, darling. You're probably worried about losing me, hence your distress and vampire phobia.'

The arrogance.

Also, my magic faded after the 'insect bite'. I never knew I had magic powers – I just thought my sunny disposition affected people positively. Since I was little, many have said my presence seems to lift gloomy atmospheres. 'The mood always lifts when you walk into a room, darling,' my favourite aunt once said.

I'd thought it was just my natural happiness that lifted moods until a beautiful spirit visited me. She said her name was Prill, and she was dead, a witch and a ghost.

'And you're a witch, also, Tuppence, and have the power to change negative atoms to positive ones. When you enter a room or area of negativity, it's like crowds of cheerful people have arrived, and it's a rare gift.'

'But I'm not a witch, just naturally happy,' I said.

'You're no longer a full witch as you're half-vampire, but I will put things right lest you become a full vampire.'

'What do you mean?'

'Gradually, your witch powers will fade, and the vampire qualities will take over, but never fear.'

Never fear? The dead woman was delusional. I had discovered I used to be a witch, my magic was fading, and I was now a half-vampire – nothing to worry about there.

I should have been terrified, but kindness shone from Prill's eyes, and she seemed sincere, well-intentioned.

Simon's eyes used to twinkle with kindness. Overnight they'd turned evil, and from being a gourmet who encouraged me to eat more – *I love a girl who loves her food* – he became puritanical. And rather than encouraging me to gain weight – *Eat this lovely chocolate cake as I like a buxom lass* – he'd wanted me skeletal.

'The wedding dress I've chosen for you won't suit a fat girl.'
How dare he?

I expected a judgmental and angry Effie to answer the door, looking haggard and worn – her not the door.

But her open face lit up in a smile of genuine welcome.

'Hello, darling girl. Come into the warm, cosy living room and let's plan your wedding.'

Cruelty in the extreme, or was poor Effie mad with grief?

I followed her into the twee floral living room, fell onto a cottage sofa and said, 'It was cruel to mention wedding arrangements now Simon is dead.'

Effie paused for dramatic effect, then said, 'No – his evil cousin is dead, but Simon is living in luxury.'

My pulse raced with hope. He couldn't be. 'Where?'

'On a yacht sailing the Greek islands. Before you say anything, he's worried sick about you and not enjoying a moment. But his death had to appear real as vampires and evil forces are after him.'

'You're lying.' *Or this is a dream.*

'No, darling, I'm not. That horrible man you've suffered for the last few months is not my darling boy, but I haven't been able to tell you until now. It was all Simon's idea – the clever lad.'

'But I can't marry Simon unless I get off a murder charge.'

The living room door opened and a familiar voice said, 'I'm sorry, miss, but you were part of a setup and MI666 is involved.'

DI Forbes, gorgeous in a red tailored skirt suit and silky black shirt, crossed the room and struck an elegant pose beside the Inglenook fireplace.

'Please explain – I don't know of MI666,' I said.

It was dreamlike, but I so wanted it to be real and Simon to be alive. Could it be true?

I crossed my fingers as DI Forbes lit a Sobranie cigarette, puffed thoughtfully, then said, 'It's a special division which deals with paranormal criminal activity. Don't divulge a word of this, apart from to Milly, who a dead witch called Prill assured me never passes on secrets.'

'How do you know I won't pass on secrets?' I asked.

DI Forbes raised a dark brow. 'You want your vampire curse reversed, don't you?'

'Of course.'

'Well, it depends on your discretion as the powers will know if you break your promise.'

After a pause for tea and shortbread, DI Forbes continued, 'We had various problems – including vampires overtaking Brighton and those awful Ratchets. The only decent member of that family is Jimmy. But a local criminal lured him into something naughty involving stolen goods a few weeks ago, so I made a deal with him – if he popped the poison into the fake Simon's coffee, we would drop some charges.'

'So who was the fake Simon?'

'His distant cousin, Silas, a vampire who was obsessed with you. He told Simon if he couldn't have you, he would kill you. Simon was terrified for your life, so together, we planned this crazy scheme. I'm Simon's aunt on his dad's side, by the way.'

'Surely there was a simpler method?' I said.

'Not really, as it's convoluted. Or perhaps my career of catching villains who make things unnecessarily complicated has rubbed off on me.'

'But Silas bit my neck, so I'm now a vampire.'

'Don't worry – we can reverse the vampire curse within three months.'

'Who is this we?'

'Oh, didn't I mention? I'm a witch and know all about Fawn's mum and Prill.'

Was everyone a witch?

'Are you a witch?' I asked Effie, who was reading *Woman's Own*.

She looked up and said, 'Oh, no, dear – a bitch, according to my ex-husband, but not a witch.'

'But you're in the police and effectively murdered someone,' I said to DI Forbes.

'Silas isn't dead – it just looked that way. We handed him to Tallon, who transported him to Transylvania for breaking the vampire code.'

'Vampires have a code?'

'All organisations have codes. Silas threatened Tallon's empire and will get his just rewards. I would not wish to be him.'

'Why involve me?'

'I'd have thought that obvious, dear.'

Perhaps I was stupid. 'No, it's not.'

'It was a cover-up for Simon's disappearance – to keep him safe while we foiled Silas and a few other dangerous people. We knew you'd be safe, Tuppence, because Silas was obsessed with your beauty.'

'I'm not beautiful.'

'I suggest you get a professional photograph taken and look at it every five years. You will eat your words.'

'Thanks – I think.'

DI Forbes pulled a gold-toned compact from her black leather handbag and refreshed her coral lipstick. 'Before the con, Silas was skinny, so we fed him lots of pasta, pizza and chocolate fudge cake and performed plastic surgery to make him more like your chubby-cheeked Simon.'

My darling teddy bear – I was so happy and would eat to my heart's content – bliss. I tried to wrap my head around everything. 'Why did Simon need to disappear?'

'I told you – to keep you safe from Silas.'

'No – there's more to it – I can tell.'

DI Forbes sighed. 'Full marks for observation. The ringleader of the local criminal underground discovered the truth.'

'What truth?'

'Everyone thinks Tarquin is the wealthiest man in Brighton, but it's Simon – he inherited it all from his grandad. Tarquin exudes charm and confidence and can spot fortune hunters and confidence tricksters a mile away. He also loves the limelight while Simon wants a cosy home, a happy wife, a roaring fire and his pipe and slippers while Tarquin fronts his businesses.'

I imagined years of contented evenings as Simon and I read by the fireside with mugs of cocoa as our children – two girls and two boys – slept upstairs. It wouldn't satisfy every woman, but it would make me happy. 'You're right. Simon likes to be low key, and Tarquin is the opposite.' *And suits flamboyant Fawn to a tee.*

'I still don't understand why anyone would harm my Simon,' I continued.

DI Forbes said, 'Because he's a threat to the greedy banking elite, some of whom are vampires and shapeshifters. The world is not as it seems.'

'Why was Simon a threat?'

'When a certain criminal nearly ruined many local people's livelihoods, Simon baled them out and created pension portfolios. The man is a financial genius.'

'My Simon?'

'Yes.'

Who knew?

'Absolutely. But a certain person wants him dead, and we're not sure if that person is connected to vampires or not.'

I buried my head in my hands as so little made sense, and I couldn't untangle all the anomalies.

'What's the matter, dear?' said Effie.

'As Simon's secretary, there seemed little going on.'

DI Forbes said, 'Tarquin's family lost everything a few years ago, and most of their apparent wealth now belongs to Simon. So, Tarquin fronts the businesses while Simon is the mastermind behind them.'

Still confused, I said, 'So why does Simon run a small estate agency?'

'Hiding in plain sight, dear. You may have noticed he only dealt with small properties?'

'Yes, I'd wondered how he managed. All we've sold this year is a florist shop and three small flats. But I still don't understand.'

Di Forbes said, 'Neither do I, and I've been at this job for years. Humans and other entities have an insane ability to complicate matters. Anyway, I must return to headquarters.'

'May I ask another question?' I said.

'Shoot.'

'Who is the criminal you suspect?'

'Another person hiding in plain sight, who has gone too far, especially with *loyal employees* who have turned informants.'

'Who is he?'

'Did I say it was a man?'

'No.'

'Then you shouldn't presume.' DI Forbes stood, brushed some invisible crumbs from her black pencil skirt, donned her chic grey coat and click-clacked from the room in a delicious cloud of Chanel No 19.

At the door, she paused and said, 'If it goes to plan, all will be revealed at the Halloween party.'

When she left, I said to Effie. 'Did you understand all that?'

'No, dear, but I'm sure things will clarify. If not, as long as we're happy in our own little worlds, who cares? Contented people are never dangerous; it's the unhappy ones who are a threat to society. Would you like a slice of freshly baked coconut cake?'

My mouth watered. 'Yes, please. But why didn't you serve it to DI Forbes.'

'Ha! That figure-obsessed skinny would have refused.'

'How silly of her – a large slice for me, please.'

'Greedy girl – I love it.'

Sinister Things

Tuppence ran into Sweetie Pie, sat with me and whispered, 'Oh, Milly, I'm so happy – Simon is alive, and I'm off the hook.'

'Shush.' I put my finger to my lips, thrilled for my daughter yet worried someone might overhear. 'Tell me all, but in a whisper.'

The information was as hard to digest as my rock-hard scone, but I was over the moon that Tuppence was innocent and Simon (the genuine version) was alive. Hopefully, the vampire reversal spell would work, and Tuppence would be safe.

But I couldn't understand why Sweetie Pie was so busy, and the phrase, *misery loves company* popped into my head.

Who could the criminal be?

Could it be Terry?

He'd already persuaded Robbie to part with the Brighton Lanes shop and all its stock.

And the Aston Martin, but perhaps it was worth less than Terry thought as Robbie seemed smug about the transaction. But was Terry small fry compared to a major criminal, or was his gregarious, helpful persona a perfect front for something sinister?

I needed a chat with Audrey, who I suspected was less gullible and pliable than Terry imagined. But Terry said she'd gone to Harrods.

'Do you know Audrey, Terry's wife?' I asked Tuppence.

'Yes.'

'What does she look like?'

'See for yourself – she's coming in.'

A tall, elegant woman, who I wouldn't match with Terry in a million years, walked towards us. She wore a chic powder-blue suit with a knee-length skirt, pillbox hat, and navy kitten heels with a matching handbag. But, despite the stylish clothes, the severe chin-length bob suggested seriousness rather than frivolity.

'Audrey,' said Tuppence, 'Come and join us.'

After small talk about the weather and local shops, Tuppence left, Audrey smiled at me, and my inference about coldness disappeared in a warm ray of golden sunlight.

'I thought you'd gone to Harrods for a Halloween outfit,' I said.

'Who told you that?'

'A little bird.'

'Ha! Terry, no doubt – he gets everywhere, especially under my skin. Anyway, I have a wardrobe full of suitable outfits and mentioned Harrods to escape him.'

'Why would you want to escape Terry?' *As if I don't know.*

'Because he's a cunning little worm.'

'Don't hold back.'

She smiled ruefully. 'I've kept it all back for too long, but there's something about you that inspires one to reveal all.'

The story of my life, not that I minded. 'If you dislike him so much, why not leave him?' Gosh – I sounded like Marjorie Proops, the agony aunt.

'Originally, it was because he threatened to take my children away, but now the youngest is eighteen, I'm safe. However, I'm biding my time, playing him at his own game. My advantage is he thinks I'm stupid, but I've been on to him for years.'

Juicy. 'Oh, do tell. Shall we order another coffee?' The cappuccinos were passable.

'Good idea – we'll pop a little brandy in.'

'They don't serve alcohol,' I said.

'No worries, I have two lipsticks.'

Lipsticks?

After the coffees arrived, Audrey took a lipstick from her Gucci handbag, removed its shiny gold top, and tipped a tot of brandy into her cappuccino.

'Lipstick, darling?' She offered a shiny pink tube.

'Don't mind if I do.' I tipped the contents of Foiled Again Fuchsia into my frothy drink.

How would Fawn react when she discovered most of Tarquin's wealth was fake, despite wishing he were poorer?

Knowing my friend, she wouldn't give a damn.

'Are you okay?' said Audrey. 'Your brow is furrowed.'

I smoothed my forehead with a hand. 'I'm fine – but there have been many uncomfortable revelations lately.'

'Hang onto your hat; there's more to come.'

'Go on...'

Audrey sipped her spiked coffee appreciatively. 'I didn't fancy Terry one bit when we met – still don't. I was seventeen, going out with a gorgeous boy named Sam Harper, and repeatedly wrote my married name in school rough books – Mrs Audrey Harper.'

With a smile, I said, 'I did the same – except I was Mrs George Harrison.'

Audrey laughed. 'Anyway, Sam Harper threw me over for a blonde with big boobs. I was heartbroken, and Terry dried my tears. One night he took me to London, and we stayed overnight in a posh hotel – the Glitz. We had a decadent dinner – oysters, champagne, steak and two bottles of Margaux.'

Whoops. I guessed what was coming next – the story as old as time.

'I was so drunk I threw caution to the wind and slept with Terry in the full sense of the word. Brought up by strict grandparents after my parents died in a car crash, I can't say the word sex.'

'You just did.'

'So I did – SEX.'

We snickered like teenage boys as the snooty waitress pursed her thin lips and glared, but Audrey ignored her and said, 'I didn't want to see Terry again, and I went back with Sam Harper – until he cheated with a sleek-haired brunette.'

'The cad,' I interjected.

'Tell me about it. And I discovered I was pregnant from my night with Terry, and my Catholic grandparents threatened a mother and baby home overseas. Terry seemed the lesser of two evils, so I married him in haste, repented at leisure.'

'Did you marry in church?'

'No – my grandparents insisted on a registry office and didn't even attend. I haven't seen them since, and they never acknowledged my son and daughter.'

'Are they still alive?'

'I doubt it.'

'How was the marriage at first?'

'Fine until I realised Terry's cheeky-chap easy ways were a veneer for a big bully.'

Inwardly shocked, I said, 'I hope he doesn't hit you.'

'Apart from the odd warning pinch or kick under the table, he's never violent but is an arch manipulator and used the children as bargaining chips from day one.'

'How many children do you have?'

'Two – a boy and a girl. Terry and I haven't slept together since we conceived our daughter and have separate bedrooms, although he pretends we do sleep together. He likes to display his elegant wife while he frolics with floozies.'

'I heard about the nude tennis,' I said.

She grinned. 'I suppose you also heard how upset I was?'

'Yes.'

'An act – couldn't give a damn. Whenever I'm upset, Terry gives me jewellery or a wad of cash to buy something – I've milked it to the hilt. He thinks I buy designer handbags and clothes, but they are all from chain stores or markets, and I change the labels and invest the cash, and now have enough to leave him. Before I do, I'll tell him I have a hidden file of his crimes and misdemeanours, and if anything happens to me – well, you can guess the rest.'

I could. 'Terry persuaded Robbie to sell his shop – said his friend wanted it.'

'Not a friend, I'm guessing – just someone who got a backhander. All the *friends who want things* are Terry's inventions. With new people the deals are good, to begin with, then he ropes them in. Brighton is full of people scared to speak out.'

'Do you know who caused the flood in Books and Bites?'

'Yes – my darling husband. He blackmailed that Ratchet boy into doing it. When they renew the carpet, Terry will probably engineer more unfortunate mishaps causing Tallon to sell the premises; at least, that's his plan. Can you guess Terry's latest story to keep me under his thumb?'

'No. What is it?'

'Vampires. He told me to stay away from Brighton Lanes as it's rife with vampires.'

'That's crazy.'

When I arrived home, Robbie pulled me into a massive bear hug. 'Oh, Milly, I'm so happy, and my life is complete.'

'Because of Prospero?'

'Partly – he's great, but because of Mum and Dad.'

'I don't understand.'

He laughed. 'No need to pretend – Mum and Dad's ghosts visited me earlier and told me everything.'

I fell onto a sofa beside Prospero and Saphira as Robbie paced the room, eyes alight with joy, too excited to sit.

Prospero had barely said a word since the day before, not even barked. Perhaps he was saving his energy, but he had a lovely friendly vibe, and I was happy we had him. Prospero was already one of the family but was obviously a sofa hog – or sofa dog.

Worried Robbie might be angry with me for the non-disclosure of his parents' status, I said, 'You're not annoyed?'

'How could I be? Mum told you not to say a word, and you didn't. It's an admirable quality. She even told me that you inherited the London flat I thought she'd rented – everything. And about your trip back in time to help solve a murder, save your daughter, and so much more. I'll call you Wonder Woman from now on, and you'd look saucy in her sexy outfit. I'm so proud of you.'

Tight tension I hadn't known I had about keeping secrets from my beloved Robbie relaxed, and my shoulders dropped from my ears to their rightful place. And I'd soon tell him about Tuppence – my oldest child. 'How did your mum realise it was safe to tell you? She was worried you'd freak out.'

He laughed. 'Families keep too many secrets and often underestimate each other. I always intuited something magical about Mum and Dad but couldn't put my finger on it, and when they died, I never believed they had truly gone. And I often smelled Mum's favourite fragrances – she was a walking perfumery department. And, at Terry's, we watched a video of a daft 1960s American sitcom, *My Mother the Car.*'

'I don't know it.'

'It's great – about the relationship between a man and his mum who reincarnates in a 1928 Porter automobile. I told Audrey I'd give anything to see Mum again, even if she haunted my cars.'

'That sitcom sounds fun.'

'It is – was.'

'I don't suppose they told you about this evening?' I said.

'Who?'

'Your Mum and Dad – Prill and Bill. Have you forgotten them already?'

Robbie swatted me playfully. 'They told me everything, even about the vampires.'

'So you know the cat can talk?'

Saphira hissed then said, 'Of course. Why would they omit the most important news?'

'How have you put up with this sassy cat?' said Robbie.

Saphira unsuccessfully tried to hide a grin, obviously thrilled to have another sparring partner.

There was at least one thing Robbie didn't realise. 'And Prospero the dog can talk,' I said.

The disbelief on Robbie's face made me and Saphira laugh.

'That flummoxed him,' said Prospero.

After a good laugh, I gave Robbie his horns and tail, and locked myself in the guest bathroom for a long, deep jasmine-scented bubble bath before slipping into my vampire dress.

When he saw me, Robbie's eyes came out on stalks. 'You look gorgeous, my sexy little vampire vixen. Show me how you bite necks.'

I did.

And more.

As I was dressing Prospero in a devil-dog outfit, Prill appeared from nowhere as usual and said, 'He doesn't need an outfit.'

'But why? It's cute.'

'The reason is a surprise.'

'I've discovered more stuff,' I continued. 'Audrey said...'

'Save it for the pre-party meeting as there's a problem in Rome that involves the Pope and a would-be imposter. I'm always so busy on All Hallows' Eve – it's the night all the charlatans, evil witches, warlocks and vampires have the most power but are at their most vulnerable.'

I was feeling pretty vulnerable myself and was worried sick about Tuppence. What if the vampire-reversal spell didn't work?

Halloween Party

Fawn and Tarquin's home, Greyspires, was a gothic Victorian mansion, perfect for spooky occasions.

Robbie and I arrived an hour before the party began, and a ghost led us to the study where a cadaverous butler served us severed fingertips (cocktail sausages dipped in tomato ketchup) and steaming glasses of hemlock cocktail. I hoped it wasn't real hemlock, but it tasted of aniseed and something earthy and delicious.

Prill and Bill floated through the cobwebbed high ceiling. It was the first time I'd seen them together in ages, and they looked terrific as old Hollywood versions of Dracula and his bride.

Prill sipped the steamy cocktail. 'Ah, I needed that – I asked you here early for a briefing – so we know what to expect. Also, to double confirm our suspicions and findings as tonight's deeds will be final and irreversible.'

Black Widow spiders crawled over my flesh as Robbie sensed my trepidation and squeezed my hand tight.

'Where's Tarquin,' I asked Fawn.

'Having a long bath – the darling thinks this is a normal party.'

But I was more interested in Tuppence's whereabouts, and Prill must have sensed my panic as she said, 'Tuppence will appear later – never fear.'

Never fear? Impossible, with my daughter's future at stake – pun not intended.

After the scary briefing, we moved to the dimly lit banquet hall, where bats hung from the vaulted ceiling, and the serving staff were dressed as ghouls. I experienced another flash of terror, but Prill had double assured us that the innocent would be safe whatever horrors ensued.

At Prospero's greedy urging, we stood by the buffet table where spiders and flies (plastic but lifelike) crawled over the food.

As The Grim Reaper (disc jockey) played 'Black Magic Woman', a stunning femme fatale in a plunge-neckline tight crimson maxi dress sashayed in with Terry. It took me a moment to realise it was Audrey, as Valeria from *Carry On Screaming*.

Robbie gave a low whistle. 'Wow, who's the hottie?'

'Terry's wife, Audrey,' I said in admiration.

'Last I saw her, she looked like a conservative MP, and Terry treated her like a servile 1950s housewife, but I reckon she's not what he believes.'

No flies on my hubby. 'Let's say hello.' I took his hand.

While Robbie and Terry chatted about cars, I admired Audrey's long ebony wig, and she said, 'That bob atrocity is a wig, but this is my real hair.'

'Does Terry know?'

'Of course not.'

Prospero appeared and held up a paw. 'You want a sausage, boy?' Robbie said.

My husband popped a sausage into the dog's willing mouth. Then another.

'Don't overfeed him,' I said, thinking Prospero's talking had been an aberration.

Wrong.

'I'm more in control of my appetite than most humans – look at him over there. Prospero bobbed his wet nose towards a large man in a sack-like skeleton outfit.

'Shush, Prospero, someone might overhear,' I hissed.

'Nothing to what they'll see and hear soon,' he growled above 'Monster Mash'.

Nervous, I looked around the room. Most invitees were there and a few extras. Some had made Halloween efforts, and others wore dark-coloured clothes without spooky embellishments. The haughty proprietor and snooty waitress from Sweetie Pie were the ugly sisters (or was that their usual party garb?), accompanied by the three men in pinstripe suits. But they'd added wizard hats in honour of the occasion.

The beautiful redhead I'd noticed in Rich and Pour wore a tight black sheath dress with a colossal diamante spider on one shoulder. I'd spotted something similar in Butler & Wilson's South Molton Street window and admired it.

Fawn, a mini-skirted witch, said, 'Mum would kill me if she saw me in this outfit as genuine witches don't wear pointy hats and stuff – that's all fairy tales.'

'Or horror stories,' I added.

Prill whispered, 'There will be a horror story soon, Milly, but don't worry.'

The more she told me not to worry, the more I worried, and my skin tingled as I said, 'Can everyone see you?'

'Only those in on the secret. Tonight, evil deeds brewing for decades will be redeemed and avenged.'

I gulped as she said, 'Don't worry, Milly, as you've done your bit. Enjoy the party, mingle, then watch truth and justice unfold.'

Needing a diversion, I grabbed Robbie's hand and pulled him onto the dance floor, where we gyrated to Creedence Clearwater Revival's 'Bad Moon Rising' as my fears subsided. By the time we'd bopped to 'Thriller', 'Werewolves of London', and 'Devil Woman', I almost forgot we were partying for any reason other than enjoyment.

At fifteen minutes to midnight, the music stopped, and Prill stood on the podium beside Bill and glared as most guests turned to stone apart from me, Fawn, Robbie, and a few others. Well, not literally stone, but they appeared immobile.

I held my breath, and even though Prill and Bill said the innocent would be safe, ropes of fear wrapped around me like poisonous, vengeful asps.

'Oy, what's going on?' said Terry.

DI Forbes mounted the podium, picked up the microphone, stared at Terry and said, 'Your demise, Terry, and it's about time as you've sabotaged Brighton's good people for years.'

Terry poked an innocent finger at his chest. 'Me? I'm a diamond geezer and only wish to help everyone.'

'Hinder them more like,' spat Audrey. 'You exploit everyone and have treated me like dirt. Your evil rule has ended, and I'm moving to Transylvania with my beloved.'

Her beloved? Who was her beloved? Prill hadn't warned me about this bit.

Audrey held out an elegant hand, and Tallon dashed towards her, kissed her long and hard on her blood-red lips. When he let her go, he said, 'Oh, my darling. I haven't been this happy since I lost the love of my life in 1896, but she was a pale imitation of you.'

I couldn't assimilate, neither could Saphira, who sprang onto my shoulder and hissed, 'Tallon's different. What happened?'

Tallon heard Saphira and said, 'I apologise about tormenting you in the 1970s, Saphira, but I was suffering from heartbreak.'

'Save it until the violinists arrive,' snapped Saphira in a light-hearted fashion, and we all, apart from Terry, laughed.

'I thought Tallon was gay and was with William?' I muttered to Robbie.

But Tallon overheard me and retorted, 'Humans are obsessed with labels. Over the centuries, I have loved both men and vomen.'

'What's going on?' Terry's sly eyes darted nervously.

Prill picked up a bell and rang it as Prospero tripled in size, pointed fangs shot from his mouth and his eyes glowed hellfire red. Terrified, I stepped back as Prospero growled, and his demonic eyes glared at Terry. 'I aim my wrath only at you – run for your life before I rip you to pieces.'

Needing no second bidding, Terry fled, pursued by the beast. Safe on the doorstep with Robbie, I watched him clamber into a Porsche, screaming in pain after Prospero's fangs took a chunk from his bony bum. Howling in pain and terror, Terry revved the engine

as the posh Porsche turned into a cute Robin Reliant and stalled to a halt as Prospero hid behind a bush.

Probably thinking Prospero had retreated, Terry left the dead car and ran against the wind as horizontal rain further hindered his pathetic progress.

The wind became a hurricane as we all cowered under a wide veranda where there was magically only a light breeze.

Prospero held back, barking just enough to terrify Terry as he limped towards the nearby wood, the wild wind and horizontal rain against him.

After a loud crunch, a large chestnut tree fell and flattened the hapless escapee.

No way could anyone survive that, and Audrey cheered. But Prospero leapt towards the three men in pinstripe suits who were cowering next to the ugly sisters.

As the terrified quintet pressed themselves against the veranda's back wall, Prospero reared up and growled in demonic tones, 'You saw what happened to your evil ringleader. Repent of your sins and reform, or you will be next.'

Then he reverted to his cute-dog incarnation.

Phew.

Indoors as the windows rattled, Fawn phoned the emergency services. 'A tree just fell and crushed a man to death. Oh, yes, I see.'

She replaced the green receiver. 'A hurricane is sweeping most of the south coast.'

'That's Michael Salmon's career blown away,' Robbie whispered.

'The poor man.' But without Terry, many of my worries had gone with the wind, but I was still concerned about the vampire problem – and Tuppence. Why wasn't she here yet? Would the vampire reversal spell work?

Prill took to the podium again. 'What you saw here tonight must remain forever a secret. Brighton has been under the thrall of an evil manipulator, and I wrongly blamed Tallon, but all vampires are not bad, and many use blood banks like supermarkets these days and harm nobody.'

Tallon said, 'Thanks for understanding, Prill. Even in the 1970s, at my vorst, it vas because of Terry's evil influence.'

'How could Terry, a mortal, have such power?' I said.

Tallon answered, 'Terry's grandmother was a dark vitch and left him a potent spell vhich allowed him to manipulate and extort vhilst his targets believed him a soft touch. It's called The Volf in Sheep's Clothing Spell.'

Prill eyed us all as if she were Jean Brodie, and we were her young charges. In my mind, I heard Geraldine McEwan say in a Scottish accent, 'Give me a girl at an impressionable age, and she is mine for life'.

Prill warned, 'Keep the revelations secret or suffer a terrible fate. Do you all understand?'

We nodded like schoolchildren.

Glaring at the trembling Sweetie Pie quintet, Prill repeated, 'Do you understand? I want to hear you say yes.'

'Yes,' they said in shaky tones.

'Good,' said Prill. 'It's not entirely your fault, as Terry had a hold over you, but you must no longer add Silajo to your baking. It is the antithesis of positive Ojalis and is very dangerous and demonic. Do you understand?

'Yes,' said Sweetie Pie's proprietor, now somewhat cowed. 'The Silago essence will be powerless without Terry's magic, anyway. And he said his magic would die with him unless he passed it on before his demise. We never wanted to do Terry's bidding anyway, but his threats and blackmail were terrible. He even...'

Prill held up a hand. 'I don't need to know – without Terry and that awful Silago, your lives will improve, and Sweetie Pie will be a happier place. Terry wanted people terrified, as fearful folks are easy to control.'

Gosh – no wonder Prill had wanted me to distribute the magic shortbread with its Ojalis essence – to counteract the negative vibes emanating from Sweetie Pie and its Silajo.

Then Prill said, 'On the bar are some blue drinks. If anyone wishes to revert their half-vampire status, drink the contents of one glass, and you will be entirely human again via a special spell effective only on Halloween.'

Where was Tuppence? Why wasn't she here? *Oh, please hurry as my heart can't take much more.*

'Vhat about full vampires?' said Tallon.

'Drink the blue liquid, and you will be only half-vampire. But for etiquette and magic reasons, it's ladies first, so please step forwards, Tuppence.'

To my indescribable relief, Tuppence suddenly appeared, hand-in-hand with the chubby Simon I'd seen in the photograph. Then she elegantly walked to the bar, ethereal and dainty, dressed as a fairy in a gossamer full-skirted grey dress.

She swallowed the magical liquid as Prill gave me a surreptitious thumbs up and I nearly swooned from relief and joy.

It was a blissful moment when Tuppence smiled, and her little fangs had retracted, and I cheered as she ran into Simon's arms.

Then William dashed to the bar, grabbed a glass, gulped down the liquid and stood with an expectant expression. Nervous on his behalf, I clutched Robbie's hand as I awaited the result. Prill had said that as William had been a vampire for a year, the reversal spell depended on him having been bitten with one fang. Which meant the perpetrator had to be Tallon. And we'd know the spell had been successful if little puffs of grey smoke emitted from his ears.

They did.

William shouted, 'I'm born again and felt that awful vampire energy leave me.'

Tallon said, 'And, you von't have to drink blood again, Villiam.'

'But I never drank b-b-b-blood,' stuttered William.

'Er, yes, you did. What did you think the *iron supplement* was?'

William clutched his throat then fainted onto a conveniently located plush sofa.

Prill eyed Audrey and said, 'You have two minutes to drink the magic blue liquid before its Halloween spell wears off. Do you wish to be fully human again?'

Audrey gazed at Tallon. 'Only if you drink it and become half-vampire.'

'Vhat do you vant, my darling?' said Tallon.

'With Terry dead and gone, perhaps we can be happy in Brighton, and I'd like to stay near my children.'

'Ve vill drink the blue liquid together, my love.'

As the rim of the glasses reached Tallon's and Audrey's lips, Prill said, 'Not so fast.'

Perplexed, the love-struck duo's panicked eyes widened in unison as Prill warned, 'If you swallow the blue liquid, Tallon, you will be reborn at age fifty and then age normally. No spell, bite or potion will make you a vampire again.'

'I thought I'd become half-vampire,' said Tallon.

'No.'

'How come?'

'Via a special spell rarely allowed by the WFGC. And, Audrey, if you don't drink it, you will become a full vampire within a month. But if neither of you drinks it, you must move to Transylvania, never to darken our doorstep again. What's it to be?'

Without hesitation, Tallon gazed into Audrey's eyes and said, 'I vish to drink the blue liquid and stay here with my beloved if that is her vish.'

Audrey's eyes glowed with happiness. 'Oh, yes, my love.'

They drank the blue liquid as Prill said, 'It's time to bring those immobilised from under my spell.'

William eyed Tallon and said, 'Does this mean I'm free to be with Phoenix?'

'Yes, of course, Villiam.'

'If he'll have me back, can we run Books and Bites together?'

Tallon frowned. 'I planned on selling it.'

Bill, Prill's husband, a solicitor when he'd been alive (sometimes now when dead), raised a grey, bushy brow. 'You and Audrey have plenty of money, Tallon, and Books and Bites is a mere drop in the ocean of your wealth. You should sign over the deeds to William as compensation for his suffering. I will draw up the paperwork.'

Tallon nodded. 'So be it.'

William shrieked and jumped up and down. 'Oh, thank you, thank you, Tallon. But why is Phoenix like a statue? I want to proposition him.'

Prill clicked her fingers as those turned to stone came to life and looked around in bewilderment.

Robbie addressed the newly mobile crowd, who all sported dazed and confused expressions. 'Don't worry – the terrible storm shocked and immobilised many of us. Unfortunately, there was an accident, and the police are coming.'

'What accident?' said the attractive redhead.

'A tree fell on Terry and killed him.'

'Terry of Terry's Trinkets?'

'Yes,' said Robbie.

Everyone cheered.

Then the room went silent as William approached Phoenix and loudly declared. 'I am free from Tallon, love you, and want to be with you. Will you have me?'

Without hesitation, Phoenix stroked William's face and said, 'Yes, sweetheart.'

'Tallon is giving me Books and Bites. Will you run the cafe while I run the book department?'

'Of course.'

'Good – with one proviso.'

'What's that?'

'We must never sell red-coloured food and drink.'

Phoenix's eyes gleamed with love. 'What about my red velvet cake, William darling?'

'I might make an exception.'

On the following Monday, I met Fawn in Rich and Pour to chat about a new business.

As we sipped cappuccinos and munched bacon sandwiches, I noticed someone had left the local paper behind, and I was thrilled to see a prominent piece on the front page.

A Public Apology

The local police wish to extend a complete apology to Miss Tuppence Brereton, wrongly arrested for murder recently. Also, they are glad to say that the victim was not Simon Shaw but a dangerous imposter. Because of ongoing investigations, they cannot divulge more.

Epilogue

December 24th, and the new boutique in Henderson's, Trendy Mums and Daughters, had been busy. When the last satisfied customers left, Fawn said, 'Shall we have a glass of fizzy apple juice before meeting everyone in the restaurant?'

Simon had taken over Luigi's, a local Italian restaurant, for a special party – his and Tuppence's wedding reception. They'd married a week earlier in Vegas, and I couldn't be happier for them.

After much discussion with Prill and Robbie, I decided not to tell Tuppence I was her birth mother – it was enough to know she was happy, and that unselfish thought assuaged much of my conscience. Besides, she'd brought her mum to our boutique for a party outfit, and when I witnessed the happy harmony between mother and daughter, I knew to leave well alone. The only extra person who knew was Robbie.

The cork popped from the bottle, and we laughed as the drink fizzed into our flutes.

'Cheers,' said Fawn. 'Here's to our new business venture. Are you glad to work in fashion again, Milly?'

'Thrilled. No more cafes for me apart from as a punter. I even visit Sweetie Pie occasionally, and those awful white walls are now a cheerful, sunny yellow.'

'What about Books and Bites?'

'Love it, and visit on my days off. The atmosphere is funky and fabulous, and William and Phoenix are adorable together. William manages the book department, and Phoenix bakes like an angel. His buttery scones and apple pies are to die for.'

'Do you miss baking the magic shortbread, Milly?'

'Not really, and Prill said there was no point now we've resolved the vampire and Terry problems, and the magic is needed elsewhere. Prill and Bill are currently dealing with problems in Parliament.'

'Ha! That might take forever.'

'Did Prospero ever tell you about his past?' Fawn said.

'Just that he was once a dog familiar to an evil warlock, wishes to forget it and be a regular dog.'

Fawn giggled. 'Yes – and regular dogs can talk.'

'He hardly speaks these days, but he and Saphira are as thick as thieves. Prill said Prospero's Halloween feat used a decade of energy, and he deserves a medal. But the other day, he told me he's happy and content, then requested sirloin steak for dinner.'

'Rex always loved his sirloin steak.'

'Is there something you haven't told me?' I'd thought Fawn's initial reaction to Prospero was odd.

'Yes – he was Mum's magic dog when I was a child. But when I was sixteen, he left us for an important mission.'

'Which was?'

'Mum never said – classified information. But she warned me that it was written in the stars for you to adopt him, and I could barely look at him initially lest my heart broke with envy.'

'You're over it now, though?'

'Of course. We love chatting about old times.'

Once a week, Prospero stayed with Fawn and Tarquin overnight – at his request, and he hadn't said why. And after a 'good romp over the downs,' Fawn delivered him home in her beloved Mercedes.

In a swathe of iridescent silver stars, Prill appeared, resplendent in a sparkly red dress, and said, 'Hello, darlings and goodbye – Bill and I are off to Barbados for Christmas.'

'Have a wonderful time, Prill. I'm so happy you and Bill decided not to move to that Nirvania place,' I said.

'So am I – we couldn't bear to – not with a grandchild imminent.'

I patted my tiny bump. The late-in-life baby was a shock but a wonderful one. How we would explain that its paternal grandparents were a witch and warlock, I had no idea.

But we'd cross that magical bridge when we came to it.

For now, I was happy with a love-child on its way, and that was enough for anyone.

And it was Christmas – time to eat, drink and be merry.

If you missed the first two books in Milly's Magical Midlife series, check them out here...

Book 1 – *Baking and Entering*[1]

Book 2 – *Scone but Not Forgotten*[2]

---

1.   *https://books2read.com/bakingandentering*

2.   *https://books2read.com/sconebutnotforgotten*

Time Travel-Guru Blurb

If you enjoyed Milly's Magical Midlife series, you'll love Scarlett King's Time-Travel Adventures. The first book in the series is Time-Travel Guru and here's the blurb...

She's about to find more than just herself...

When Scarlett's bossy fiancé of six years asks her to move to spooky Mystic Manor, her intuition screams no. But he always gets his way. Unwillingly ensconced in the new house, she discovers a not-so-friendly ghost.

It's the final nail in the relationship coffin and Scarlett flees to a Find Yourself seminar. There, the heart-stopping handsome course leader is the perfect balm for her wounded heart. But he asks Scarlett to join him on a risky time-travel journey.

Mission? To rescue a renowned Indian guru from the clutches of money-mad mobsters.

Can Scarlett believe the crazy time-travel story, or is it a corny chat-up line? But maybe she should cast doubt aside, and risk all in the name of love.

Not all that glitters is groovy in this romantic comedy which is totally far out.

<u>Get Time-Travel Guru here</u>[1]

Extract from Time-Travel Guru

Scarlett King – March 2018

The first sight of Mystic Manor in Lower Coffin, Surrey, gives me goosebumps. I grasp my fiancé's hand and whisper, 'Peregrine, let's go.'

'Don't be daft, Scarlett. The house you like is five hundred grand cheaper.'

Sounds odd, doesn't it? But I'm engaged to a trust-fund kid, and the trustees allotted him two million pounds to spend on a home, and Peregrine wants every penny of it. You could buy ten of my parents' semi-detached in Liverpool for the same price. I pull him back on the gravel pathway. 'The house next door is full of light and has a happy vibe.'

Peregrine mutters through his teeth, 'But it's way cheaper.'

'Yes, a snip at one and a half million,' I quip. 'Anyone can afford that.'

We're in a mental and physical tug of war. Peregrine ushers me toward the black front door and rings the bell. I await the proverbial creepy tall butler. The door creaks open. I paint a smile on my face, which turns to a gasp of horror – a slathering Rottweiler lurches towards me. I close my eyes, grasp Peregrine's hand, and wait for evil fangs to rip me apart.

'Get back!' shouts a male voice.

I think he's talking to me and would gladly oblige, but when I dare open my eyes a portly man with a tomato-red face has the evil beast by the collar. 'Don't worry; Killer is a pussycat.'

Killer? How endearing. I christen the man *Redface.*

'Why didn't he bark?' I say. There was no early warning system.

'The poor baby is hoarse from barking at the new postman.' Redface strokes Killer's back.

A skinny woman with a fox-like face, above which perches a rock-solid shampoo and set, circa the 1950s, appears. 'For God's sake, dear, stop terrifying people with that dog. I'll lock him in the utility room, while you take our guests through to the kitchen. The coffee is percolating.'

I adore coffee, and it lifts my mood. Not in this case, the divine aroma of good beans doesn't detract from my sense of impending doom.

Even the freshly baked Victoria sponge at the centre of the pine refectory table doesn't lift my spirits, although the vanilla fragrance makes my tummy do hungry somersaults.

'Do you want coffee and cake now, or shall we wait until I've shown you around?' asks Foxface.

'Now, please,' I say, hungry and wishing to delay the Amityville tour.

'After we've viewed the property,' says Peregrine.

Traitor.

His eager face shows I've lost another battle – he's mentally bought this horrid dwelling, while I adore the house next door, Wisteria Villa, which I viewed last week. As soon as I stepped over the threshold, my body went weightless with happiness. I told Peregrine about it and he wouldn't even look at the particulars, due to the lower price. Bonkers. Once again, my opinion doesn't count – money always comes first. I'm close to breaking point.

'Shall I show you around?' Redface asks.

Foxface tuts. 'No, dear, you talk too much. I'll do it – you make those phone calls and join us for coffee and cake.'

I can see who wears the trousers. Note to self – ask Foxface for lessons.

As we start the tour, I imagine I'm Mrs de Winter from Daphne du Maurier's *Rebecca,* and Foxface is Mrs Danvers.

First stop; the living room. Perhaps I overreacted – it's large and well proportioned, but not much light creeps through the small-paned windows despite the sun. What will it be like on a gloomy day?

The dismal mahogany-panelled dining room with gilt-framed paintings of solemn Victorians on the burgundy walls would be perfect for a séance or Halloween dinner. Even without guests, the room has the aura of a strained dinner party. One of those stuffy gatherings where everyone makes polite chit-chat, terrified of saying the wrong thing.

I'm not a fan of house tours unless it's a stately home, something magnificent, so I won't describe the place in too much detail. However, the building breathes evil from every nasty nook and creepy cranny.

My mood doesn't improve as we meander through the labyrinth of rooms. The house is a mishmash of styles. An original seventeenth-century manor house, with Regency and Victorian extensions, according to the details.

Each room 'enjoys' various levels of spookiness, but the worst is a bedroom and ensuite, in the oldest section. It reeks of damp, the walls are covered in stained brown hessian, the carpet is a dirty beige shag pile, and moth-eaten velvet curtains hang limply at the windows. Lovely. When I step into the claustrophobic bathroom, the hair at the nape of my neck lifts, and I understand the phrase *someone walked over my grave.* I shiver with the cold which is weird as the other rooms felt warm – and seemed in good, albeit dreary, decorative order. Surreptitiously, I put my hand on a radiator and almost need a skin graft.

We don't linger, and Foxface leads the way down a blue-carpeted corridor and opens a pink-panelled door.

'This is our pride and joy. Behold the sixth bedroom and master suite,' says Mrs Danvers, I mean Foxface.

'It doesn't fit with the rest of the house,' says Peregrine.

I gasp. The enormous room is beautiful – cream Osborne and Little curtains with a pink rose print, plush cream carpet, a king-size four-poster bed – draped with fabric to match the curtains. Another pink door leads to a huge bathroom/dressing room with a round sunken jacuzzi bath, double sink unit and a long wall of fitted wardrobes.

'Ooh, it's divine,' I exclaim.

And it feels okay – not spooky.

I have a cosy oasis – perhaps I'll cope.

The tour ends in the cluttered garage. 'Where does that door go?' I say.

Foxface clears her throat. 'To a corridor which leads to a ballroom which you can't enter, it's not safe. But the door to the ballroom has a large glass panel you can look through.'

Peregrine's eyes gleam with greed. 'It wasn't on the details. Why isn't it safe?'

'Hasn't been renovated for some time,' murmurs Foxface.

'Can we go through?' I'm enthusiastic for the first time today.

'Yes, my husband and I will wait here,' says Foxface, emulating the Queen so well she could be cast as Elizabeth the Second in *The Crown*. 'But it's at your own risk.'

At the end of the dingy corridor, Peregrine peeks through the door. 'This will make a perfect extra garage and workshop – I'll be able to add to my car collection. I've seen a super classic E-Type.'

I tut. 'For God's sake, Peregrine. You already have three cars. How many does one man need?'

'As many as possible, they're my hobby.'

'Why not choose stamps or coins? Or add to your treasured Toby Jug collection?' I peer through the grimy glass as my heart races.

The large room has as many cobwebs as Miss Havisham's drawing-room, the vintage wallpaper is damp and peeling, the wooden floor is green with slime, and the ceiling slopes downwards. However, in my mind's eye, elegant women in ball gowns and handsome men in tuxedos waltz to 'The Blue Danube' under sparkling crystal chandeliers. The potential is obvious.

I say, 'Over my dead body will you turn this into a garage. I'll only agree to live here if you promise to restore this wonderful room to its former glory.'

Peregrine pouts. 'But it's ideal for my cars.'

'I mean it. I refuse to move here unless we refurbish this heavenly space.'

'It'll be far too expensive.'

And classic cars are so cheap. 'It could pay for itself – make a fabulous wedding venue. We'll rake it in,' I say with manipulative intent. Peregrine has taught me well.

To be fair, my fiancé is kind (mostly) but ambitious for more and more wealth. His eyes flash like a one-armed bandit hitting a Las Vegas million-dollar jackpot. 'Would you organise the weddings, Scarlett?'

'Yes.'

'Okay – I'll do a deal with the sellers. Make an excuse to wait in the car – you know how embarrassed you get when I negotiate.'

He calls it negotiating, but I call it sailing too close to the wind.

Back in the car, I realise I didn't get my Victoria sponge.

Peregrine always gets his cake and eats it.

On an overcast day in May, we move into Mystic Manor. I hope I overestimated my original fear.

No.

Dread descends as I step over the threshold with none of the excitement moving to a 'better' home usually creates. I want to flee back to our (Peregrine's) now-sold terraced house in Putney.

A removal man says, 'Where do you want this box, love?'

I sigh. 'In the kitchen.' It has *kitchen* written on four sides in thick black marker pen.

'Any chance of a cup of tea, love?'

'Yes, find a box marked *kettle, tea, sugar, coffee and cups.*' I've been that organised – to detract myself from hideous imaginings about Mystic Manor. 'I'll nip to the local shop for milk.'

As I dawdle down the path, Peregrine tears after me. 'They've only been here for ten minutes, for God's sake. Why are you making tea?'

I look skywards. 'Why not? They're being paid for the job, not by the hour. Who cares how long they take?' *Forever would be good.*

The shopkeeper, a sharp-eyed petite woman, hands me a flimsy, transparent white carrier bag. 'There you are, Scarlett. You're spoiling those removal men with chocolate Hobnobs. Welcome to our village.'

'How do you know my name?'

She raises her eyebrows. 'You obviously aren't used to small communities, but you're brave.'

'What do you mean?'

'Erm... nothing. Have a good day.'

Bile rises in my throat, and my heart beats faster. Half of me wants to know, half prefers happy ignorance.

The removal men demolish the packet of Hobnobs in one sitting.

'Right,' I say, 'Peregrine is getting antsy. If you speed things up, we'll stand you a meal in the Dog and Duck when you've finished, plus a nice fat tip.'

'Now you're talking, love,' says the chubbier of the two – I secretly nickname them Laurel and Hardy.

By six o'clock, most of the boxes and furniture are in their rightful places. My tummy rumbles.

Peregrine is unpacking his beloved Toby Jug collection – hideous things. 'Let's all go to the pub. The men have worked hard,' I say out of Laurel and Hardy's earshot.

'I want to get everything unpacked.'

I have a trump card. 'Jam roly-poly and custard is on the specials.' I went for a sneaky stroll earlier.

Peregrine puts down a Toby Jug so fast I fear for its life. He licks his lips. 'Lead the way.'

Laurel and Hardy located, I say, 'Pub?' and they need no second bidding.

The Dog and Duck, with its roaring fire, horse brasses and plush red seats has a homey vibe. At least there's a cosy refuge not far away from the creepy house.

It's lovely to relax, and the atmosphere between the four of us is convivial, plenty of teasing banter. Although Peregrine has always enjoyed a life of privilege, he is no snob – his ambition is for business and monetary gain, not social standing.

'Are you happy working for Shifters?' Peregrine asks Laurel and Hardy.

'Yes, mate,' they chorus.

Peregrine leans towards them. 'Why not start your own company? Within three years you'll have, let's see, at least five lorries and fifteen men working for you.'

'Don't want the stress, mate,' says Hardy.

'It'll be fun.' Peregrine fishes his maroon Montblanc biro from his pocket and writes figures on a red paper napkin. 'If you begin with this capital and get this loan...'

Hardy hides a yawn and Laurel's eyes glaze over.

Not another big-business lecture. Last month Peregrine tried to persuade our window cleaner to start a chain of When I'm Cleaning Windows. 'I'm happy with my one van, ladder, and bucket,' the poor man said, backing away.

Pudding arrives, saving Laurel and Hardy from death by boredom.

The hot sponge, oozing jam, is smothered in custard – we grab our spoons, and a temporary silence ensues.

At 9 pm, tipsy and full, we stagger back to Mystic Manor. It's obvious neither Laurel nor Hardy are fit to drive, so we usher them into the living room while we make coffee in the kitchen.

'We can't let either of them drive in that state,' I whisper. 'It's our fault they're pissed as farts – we kept ordering another bottle.'

Peregrine sneers. 'Nobody made them drink.'

'Don't be such a prig. They can stay over.'

Like a bird of prey, Peregrine spots an opportunity. 'And it's Saturday – Shifters is closed tomorrow – they can stay the night then help out tomorrow morning. Then Sunday lunch at the Dog and Duck.'

'We'll be back at square one, they'll be permanent guests. It'll be like *Groundhog Day*.'

Peregrine smirks. 'Nah, they have a removal to do on Monday.'

We serve coffee – laced with brandy.

At 10 am the next morning, Laurel and Hardy appear in the kitchen, bleary-eyed.

'The smell of bacon woke us.' Laurel pats his tummy.

Peregrine, his mouth too full to speak, gestures towards the table.

'Bacon butties?' I ask. Thank goodness the local shop opens early on Sundays.

'Wouldn't say no. Then we'll get on, but did you know you've got a ghost?' Hardy says.

Instead of heading to the fridge, I fall onto a chair. 'Did you see it?'

'Her – common knowledge in these parts – an old lady dressed in black – killed her husband and his lover in the 1940s and then committed suicide. She haunts the place, gun in hand, an evil expression on her face. People hear her false teeth click before they see her.'

I put my hands over my ears.

Peregrine turns ashen. 'You're making this up.'

'No, I'm not,' says Hardy.

'Where did the murders happen?' My tummy churns.

'This house.'

I curse Hardy's obtuseness. 'I realise that, but what room?'

'The spooky one with the hessian wallpaper.' Hardy confirms my fears then hands the scare-the-newcomers baton to his partner.

Laurel slurps his strong PG Tips tea with its *dash of milk and three sugars*. 'Not many stay the night in this house without being scared half to death. Your master bedroom and the living room below is a recent mock-Regency extension, and rumour says it's the only non-haunted area.'

My tummy clenches. 'But you stayed here last night.'

'Nah, we slept in the back of the lorry on a mattress. Left the front door on the latch to access the bog,' says Hardy.

'I peed in the garden,' adds Laurel.

Peregrine laughs, despite the situation. Nothing fazes him, and if he was marooned on a faraway island without a penny, he would be a millionaire within a year. He envisages only success but is blind to other people's stress, especially mine.

I doubt Peregrine will leave the house, despite the ghost – he'll use an exorcist or something, having seen the ballroom potential. However, I've had enough – no longer will he include me in his drama when my intuition screams a loud *NO*. Financially, he always wins – but the process is torturous – for me. Let him torment someone else.

It's not as if we're married, although we've been engaged for six years. Six! My fiancé is Peregrine Pratt and I'm Scarlett King. I no longer want to be a Pratt. My parents will be pleased – they can't stand him. 'He's so fake, love,' Mum often says.

I also have a hunch Peregrine is cheating on me – let her have him – let her see the dark side of this ruthlessly ambitious man. Or perhaps she's too lovelorn to notice. I don't care anymore. After ten years together and repeated dramas, all to do with Peregrine's ambition, I have nothing left, no positive resources. We have no children to stay together for the sake of – Peregrine wants to wait until we're married. It's all about Peregrine.

Enough is enough – I'm done.

And I know where I'll go to heal...

Because I'm not staying in this haunted horror...

Carry on reading Time-Travel Guru[1]

---

1.   https://books2read.com/timetravelguru

About the Author

Thank you for reading this book.

I hope you enjoyed it as much as I loved writing it. If so, if you could spare a few moments to leave a quick review on the relevant bookseller site, I would be most grateful.

Please visit my website to discover more of my fun books (link below). While you're there, I'd love you to sign up for my newsletter, Janet's VIP Readers, so you don't miss out on new releases, freebies and offers.

Thanks again.

Janet xx

Read more at www.janetbutlermale.co.uk.

Printed in Great Britain
by Amazon

14844689R00099